W9-CSH-091

"You're the new deputy?"

Deputy Halley Robinson had told herself that after moving back to Whitehorse, sooner or later she was going to cross paths with Colton Chisholm. When she'd left Whitehorse after junior high school, hadn't she sworn that one day she would return and make Colton sorry?

But that had been a young girl's dream of revenge. Halley was no longer that young, impressionable girl.

"Colton," she said, secretly enjoying the fact that he'd remembered her. "So, why don't you tell me what the problem is. You told the dispatcher you'd found Jessica Granger's purse and you believe something might have happened to her?"

"It's Jessica's. I found it at a spot we used to meet."

She raised her gaze to his. "A *secret* spot, the dispatcher said."

Colton rubbed the back of his neck. His hair was longer than she'd ever seen it. That was probably why she hadn't remembered the color, a combination of ripe wheat and sunshine that brought out the gold flecks in his brown eyes.

She felt that old quiver inside as her gaze met his. Colton Chisholm had been adorable in grade school. It shouldn't have surprised her that he'd grown into a drop-dead good-looking man.

USA TODAY Bestselling Author

B.J. DANIELS

BRANDED

™ Harlequin®

TORONTO NEW YORK LONDON
AMSTERDAM PARIS SYDNEY HAMBURG
STOCKHOLM ATHENS TOKYO MILAN MADRID
PRAGUE WARSAW BUDAPEST AUCKLAND

I wanted to kick off this new series with a dedication to a good friend who has been in my thoughts.
This one is for Debra Webb, one of the strongest, most determined women I know and one heck of a writer.

ISBN-13: 978-0-373-74597-5

BRANDED

Recycling programs for this product may not exist in your area.

Copyright © 2011 by Barbara Heinlein

Printed in U.S.A.

ABOUT THE AUTHOR

USA TODAY bestselling author B.J. Daniels wrote her first book after a career as an award-winning newspaper journalist and author of thirty-seven published short stories. Since then she has won numerous awards, including a career achievement award for romantic suspense and many nominations and awards for best book. Daniels lives in Montana with her husband, Parker, and two springer spaniels, Spot and Jem. When she isn't writing, she snowboards, camps, boats and plays tennis. To contact her, write to B.J. Daniels, P.O. Box 1173, Malta, MT 59538 or email her at bjdaniels@mtintouch.net. Check out her website at www.bjdaniels.com.

Books by B.J. Daniels

HARLEQUIN INTRIGUE

996—SECRET OF DEADMAN'S COULEE*
1002—THE NEW DEPUTY IN TOWN*
1024—THE MYSTERY MAN OF WHITEHORSE*
1030—CLASSIFIED CHRISTMAS*
1053—MATCHMAKING WITH A MISSION*
1059—SECOND CHANCE COWBOY*
1083—MONTANA ROYALTY*
1125—SHOTGUN BRIDE‡
1131—HUNTING DOWN THE HORSEMAN‡
1137—BIG SKY DYNASTY‡
1155—SMOKIN' SIX-SHOOTER‡
1161—ONE HOT FORTY-FIVE‡
1198—GUN-SHY BRIDE**
1204—HITCHED!**
1210—TWELVE-GAUGE GUARDIAN**
1234—BOOTS AND BULLETS‡‡
1240—HIGH-CALIBER CHRISTMAS‡‡
1246—WINCHESTER CHRISTMAS WEDDING‡‡
1276—BRANDED+

*Whitehorse, Montana
‡Whitehorse, Montana: The Corbetts
**Whitehorse, Montana: Winchester Ranch
‡‡Whitehorse, Montana: Winchester Ranch Reloaded
+Whitehorse, Montana: Chisholm Cattle Company

CAST OF CHARACTERS

Colton Chisholm—He has a lot to learn about first love, especially when one of his turns up again after so many years.

Halley Robinson—The new deputy in town has an old grudge to settle with the first boy she ever loved—who is also a murder suspect.

Jessica Granger—She was a master at secrets and deception, right to the end.

Hoyt Chisholm—He's been running from his past for years now, but it is about to catch up to him.

Emma McDougal Chisholm—The new bride is in for a surprise when it comes to her husband.

Aggie Wells—The former insurance investigator always gets her man and that man is Hoyt Chisholm.

Dawson Chisholm—The most serious and oldest of the boys Hoyt Chisholm adopted.

Marshall Chisholm—The second oldest is also the largest and, in his opinion, the good son of Hoyt Chisholm.

Zane Chisholm—He's the brother the other five go to when they want something done.

Logan Chisholm—He's the blond, blue-eyed wild one of the bunch of brothers.

Chapter One

Emma Chisholm heard the ruckus from clear back in the ranch kitchen. She wiped her hands on her apron as she walked toward the front of the sprawling house to peer out over the wide porch to the yard.

After a whirlwind courtship and marriage, she hadn't been prepared for her new home. Hoyt had warned her that his ranch was in the middle of Nowhere, Montana, but she hadn't been able to imagine anything this isolated or this huge.

She remembered thinking that day two weeks ago, when they'd driven north for three hours after picking up one of his ranch trucks at the airport in Billings, that she didn't really know what she was getting into—not with her new life. Or her new husband. After all, what did she really know about Hoyt Chisholm?

And what did he know about her? Very little since she had purposely skimmed over the past. It was a given that both being over fifty, they had things in their pasts they wanted to forget.

The thought that Hoyt might also have something in his past he wanted to hide had never occurred to her. That was an unsettling thought, she realized as she headed for the front of the rambling ranch house.

Even through the cloud of dust they were kicking up, she recognized the two young men brawling by the corral. Emma sighed, shaking her head as she watched two of her stepsons fighting. When Hoyt had told her that he had six sons, she'd been shocked. Funny how that hadn't come up when they met in Denver and found themselves flying to Vegas for an impromptu wedding.

She'd expected them to be boys, since that was what he called them. To her surprise, they were six grown men from twenty-six to thirty-three years old. But they definitely behaved like boys. Her six, big, strapping stepsons were typically involved in one squabble or another on a daily basis and she'd come to realize that Hoyt was usually the reason. The boys, all adopted, had apparently been raised without a woman in the house to give them any guidance and Hoyt dang sure wasn't providing any.

Emma saw her husband standing in the

shade at the other end of the porch watching two of his sons rassle in the dirt.

"You just going to stand there, Hoyt Chisholm?" she asked as she stepped out on the porch.

He shot her that grin that had stolen her heart and clearly her senses, as well. How else could she explain marrying a man she barely knew to come to this ranch so far from civilization?

Hoyt took off his Stetson and scratched the back of his neck. She could tell that he wasn't going to do a darn thing about this. Just as she could see that he wanted her to accept the way things were on the Chisholm Cattle Company ranch. By now he must be realizing that wasn't going to happen.

Stepping off the porch, she walked around to the water faucet at the side of the house, snatched up the hose and turned the faucet on full force.

Hoyt, seeing what she was up to, quickly abandoned the porch as if he just remembered he had something to do in the barn.

Emma was tempted to turn the water on him, but she knew it wouldn't do any good. He'd just laugh and hightail it out of range.

His two sons were still rolling around in the dirt as Emma dragged the hose over and sprayed them.

"What the hell?" Colton said as he leaped to his feet.

"Don't you be using that kind of language around me, Colton Chisholm," Emma snapped and sprayed him again.

Tanner was on his feet, same as his brother, both now soaked to the skin, the dust on their clothes turning to mud.

Emma shook her head as she looked at the two of them and their hangdog expressions. Both were handsome to a fault.

"This is all your doing, Hoyt Chisholm," she called after her husband. "You're the reason they're always squabbling, each of them trying to win favor with you." She'd seen *that* within the first twenty-four hours of moving into the main house even though the "boys" had their own houses on the huge ranch that was Chisholm Cattle Company.

Of course, Hoyt pretended not to hear, but she could tell by the way he ducked his head as he stepped into the barn that he'd heard just fine. His sons were brought up wild. And he thought that was a good thing?

She turned her attention back to the two young men standing before her. They had both retrieved their hats and stood looking sheepish and wet and worried about what she might do next.

"I'd best not catch you fighting like tomcats again," she said, scowling at the two of them. "Now get on out of here before I give you another good soaking."

They tipped their hats and took off in the direction their father had gone. But within a few feet she could hear them arguing again.

She shook her head. It was time for Hoyt's "boys" to grow up, and she knew exactly what each of them needed. A woman.

Not just any woman. It took a special woman to domesticate a Chisholm man, she reflected, thinking of Hoyt.

As she turned off the water and coiled up the hose again, she told herself the hardest part would be finding the right woman for each of them. Since marrying Hoyt, she'd been thinking about how to bring this family together. It was clear that her stepsons had been more than surprised when their father had brought home a wife—and less than pleased. But she was determined to change all that.

She'd have to be careful, though, Emma thought, as she turned back to the kitchen and the apple pies she was helping the cook make for supper. If Hoyt or her stepsons got wind of what she was up to, there would be hell to pay.

But she was willing to take that chance. She

smiled, thinking of her husband. The key was gentling a man, not breaking him. Love could accomplish the most amazing things, she told herself, hoping that was true.

She set her mind to which of her stepsons would be first to have his life changed forever with her help—and possibly a cattle prod.

COLTON CHISHOLM WIPED BLOOD from his split lip as he limped to his pickup. He told himself he'd gotten the best of the fight, but as he slid behind the wheel, he felt the pain in his ribs and wasn't so sure about that.

As he started the engine and roared down the road away from the ranch, he thought about just striking out and leaving Whitehorse and the Chisholm Cattle Company behind. He had plenty of reason most days.

But when he glanced in his rearview mirror, he knew he could no more leave this land than he could quit fighting his brothers for it. He was as much a Chisholm as the rest of them and he wouldn't be pushed out.

Not that his father didn't have him thinking twice about it, though. Everyone in six counties was talking about how Hoyt Chisholm had gone to the cattleman's convention in Denver and brought home a wife. And not just any wife. Emma McDougal Chisholm—a fifty-something buxom redhead with green eyes and a temper.

"The damn fool," Colton said to himself. What made it worse was that his father was plainly head over heels in love with the woman. And Emma...well, she seemed set on changing things on the ranch. He shook his head. Emma McDougal Chisholm had no idea what she'd signed on for. If she did, she'd be hightailing it out of town before sundown.

As Colton neared the highway on the long dirt road out of the ranch, he saw the postman, Albert Raines, pull up to the huge mailbox marked *Chisholm*. Albert waved to him and Colton slowed, pulling alongside as the postman got out and walked toward his pickup.

"Got a bunch of mail as usual," the tall, skinny postman said. "I was told to see that you got this personally, though." He handed Colton an envelope from the Postal Service.

At first he thought the postman was joking with him. "This about some new stamp designs?"

"Nope," Albert said with all seriousness. "It's a letter addressed to you that got lost. I brought it special."

"Thanks." He tossed it on the seat. He'd gotten other mail that had been caught in some machine and mangled and had ended up in an envelope just like the one Albert had handed him. No doubt it was a bill of some sort, since Colton rarely received anything else.

"Aren't you going to open it?" Albert sounded disappointed. "I heard it's been lost for fourteen years."

Colton chuckled. "I'm sure it will keep if it's been lost that long." He waved goodbye as he left and headed down the road to his house. He'd taken over one of the houses when his father had purchased a neighboring ranch a few years back. The house needed work, but Colton had needed space.

While the Chisholm ranch house was huge and rambling, it wasn't big enough for him and his brothers. All of them had moved out when they'd heard about their father's marriage, but they all still returned to the main ranch house for meals. Emma had seen to that.

After cleaning up, Colton headed into Whitehorse, anxious to get his errands done and get back for dinner. Emma had announced that she and the cook were baking apple pies. The way his brothers put away food, the pies wouldn't last long. Emma demanded that they all sit down to dinner each evening at the huge log dining room table at the ranch.

Crossing Emma had proved to be a bad thing, he thought, smiling at the memory of her turning the hose on him and Tanner. Emma wasn't very tall, but she was feisty as a badger—and just as dangerous when she was riled up. He figured that was one reason his father had fallen for her—and the reason this marriage didn't stand a chance in hell.

It wasn't until later, after picking up supplies, stopping to see if his saddle was fixed yet and having a cup of coffee while he waited at the local café, that Colton climbed back in his pickup and saw the envelope.

He thought about just tossing it. What was the point in looking at a bill that had gotten lost in the mail years ago? Hell, fourteen years ago he'd been eighteen, too young to have bills and who would have sent him a letter?

Curious now, he tore open the envelope and dumped out the contents.

A once-white small envelope tumbled out on his pickup seat. The moment he saw her handwriting, his heart stuttered in his chest and he found himself heaving for breath, the effort almost doubling over from the pain of his banged-up ribs. He stared at the handwriting, the return address and finally the postmark. The letter had been mailed fourteen years ago in May—right before Jessica left Whitehorse without even saying goodbye and he'd never seen her again.

He felt the heartbreak as if it had been only yesterday as he carefully eased open the back flap and took out the handwritten letter inside.

Colton,
I'm sorry we fought. But I can't stay here at the house any longer. It's only getting worse. I'm running away. I hope you'll come with me. I'll be waiting for you at our special place Friday night at midnight. If you love me, you'll meet me there and we'll go together. I have a surprise for you and can't wait to tell you.
Love,
Jessica

Colton felt as if his heart had been ripped out of his chest all over again. He let out a howl of pain as he reread the words. Jessica hadn't just taken off without a word. She'd sent this letter. Only he hadn't gotten it.

They'd had a fight the day before she left school, left Whitehorse, left him. He had been beside himself. He'd even braved going over to her house, knowing the reaction he'd get from her father.

Sid Granger had answered the door, his wife, Milli, behind him. "What the hell are you doing here? Haven't you done enough, you son of a—" His wife had grabbed his arm, trying to hold him back, but she was no match for her husband.

Sid had grabbed a baseball bat and chased him out to his pickup. "Jessica's gone and if I ever see your face around here again, I'll kill you."

In the days following, Colton had called the house, begging Sid to tell him where Jessica had gone. But the phone calls had ended with angry words and the slamming down of the receiver. They blamed *him* for Jessica leaving? He couldn't understand why. She'd loved him. It was whatever was going on at home that had made her run away.

A few weeks later, he'd seen Mrs. Granger coming out of the Whitehorse Post Office.

"Please. Tell me where she's gone," Colton had pleaded.

"Go away." Millie Granger had glanced around as if she was afraid Sid would find out she'd talked to him. "Jessica's gone. She isn't coming back. And even if she was, she wouldn't want anything to do with you."

Colton hadn't believed it at first. He'd been inconsolable for weeks.

"She obviously wasn't the right woman for you," his father finally said after watching him mope around. "Trust me, her leaving is the best thing that could have happened. You both were too damn young to be so serious."

As weeks had turned into months, Colton had been forced to accept that the first woman he'd ever loved no longer wanted anything to do with him.

Now he stared at the letter and understood what had happened, why she'd never tried to contact him. She'd reached out to him, gone to their secret spot that night, only to have him fail to show.

How long had she waited for him, thinking he would come for her? The thought of her alone there that night, waiting for him, broke his heart all over again. He couldn't bear that she'd gone away believing he hadn't loved her, that he wouldn't have been there for her. He had promised to take care of her, look out for her, and when she'd needed him, he hadn't been there.

I never got the letter.

He hadn't been to their special place for fourteen years—not since their fight and her disappearance from his life. As he drove out of town toward the ranch, he remembered the times they'd met there in secret. He would spread a blanket out for them beneath a stand of huge old cottonwood trees alongside the creek.

Even after all these years, he could remember the sound of the breeze in the leaves overhead, the sweet scent of the wild grasses, the cool coming up off the creek, the heat of her body against his.

It was in the shade of those trees that he'd first told her he loved her. They'd both been seventeen the first time they'd made love under that tree. It had been the first for both of them. Jessica had cried afterward and told him he would always be the only one for her. He'd told her he'd never let anyone hurt her again.

Colton drove past the Granger place, glancing in the direction of the house, as he had done for the last fourteen years. The house was set back off the road, almost hidden in a stand of trees. He never passed it without thinking of Jessica.

As he drove by the barbed-wire fence that marked the end of the Granger property and the beginning of Chisholm land, he slowed. Seeing no other vehicles coming down the road from either direction, he pulled in, stopping short of the barbed-wire gate.

The gate into this part of the Chisholm ranch property was seldom if ever used. The barbed wire had cut deep into the wooden posts, a sure sign that no one had been back in years. Once opened, he drove through the gate, then got out and closed it behind him.

The way in could hardly be called a road. It was a dirt path through some rugged terrain. Grass grew up between the two ruts, scraping the underside of his pickup as he drove until he reached the creek and the path petered out.

Parking in a gully where his pickup couldn't be seen from either the road or the Granger property, he walked the rest of the way, following the creek—just as he'd done as a teenager on his way to meet Jessica.

That night Jessica would have sneaked out of her parents' house and taken the back way, along the creek and through the barbed-wire fence onto Chisholm property, following the creek to the secret meeting place.

It had been Jessica who'd found the spot one night after a fight with her father. She'd wandered down the creek bank for half a mile to an oxbow surrounded by tall trees. She'd crawled through the barbed-wire fence onto Chisholm land—and realized she'd found the perfect place for them to meet in secret, her father being none the wiser.

Colton slowed his steps as he saw the tops of the trees in the distance and remembered the anticipation he'd felt each time he was to meet her all those years ago.

When he saw their secret spot, he stopped short. Jessica Granger had been his first real girlfriend, although they'd been forced to keep it secret because of her father. Sid Granger didn't want his daughter having anything to do with those wild Chisholm boys and no matter what Colton did, he couldn't convince him otherwise.

The spot didn't look as if anyone had been here in the past fourteen years since the land was posted and no one else had reason to come here. As he walked to the trees, stopping in the cool shade, he realized that the last person to stand here had probably been Jessica. His heart lodged in his throat at the thought.

For a moment he swore he caught a whiff of her perfume. The scent took him back. He could close his eyes and feel her in his arms as they lay entwined in the shade of these cottonwoods after making love.

I have a surprise for you and can't wait to tell you. Whatever it had been, he would never know, he thought as he looked around.

What the hell are you doing here? He pulled off his Stetson and raked his fingers through his sandy-blond hair. Did he think he was going to find Jessica waiting for him here? He laughed at the absurdity of it.

Hell, he couldn't even be sure she ever came here that night. Maybe she'd changed her mind, sorry she'd written him the letter, and had taken off on her own.

With a start, he remembered that Sid Granger had called the ranch that night.

"It's Granger," his father had said after answering the phone in the middle of dinner all those years ago. "He wants to know if you've seen his daughter." Colton had given his father a miserable shake of his head. "He hasn't seen her. They broke up."

He'd never seen Jessica again.

If only he'd gotten the letter, he thought angrily. He would have run off and married her in a heartbeat.

Colton took one last look at the spot under the trees. "I'm so sorry, Jessica," he whispered on the warm spring breeze rustling the leaves on the branches over his head.

A part of him ached for what could have been. They would have run away together. He could have gotten a job on a ranch. She could have gotten a job cooking for the hired hands. Or maybe he would have made enough that she didn't have to work, especially if they'd gotten a place to live along with his job.

He sighed, realizing that they had both been kids back then. The chances of his getting hired on some ranch would have been slim. Not only that, Jessica didn't know how to cook and she would have gone crazy living on a ranch. She'd always yearned to kick the dust of Montana off her heels and live in some big city. She had this idea that she would be a model. Or even a movie star.

"I'm going to be famous someday," she used to say. "You'll look back and say, 'I knew her when she was a girl.'" It used to make him sad when she talked that way because he knew he would never leave Montana.

What would he have done if he'd gotten the letter?

He would have figured something out, he told himself. He'd have had to. With her family being the way they were, he was all she had. She depended on him.

As he started to turn away, his boot toe caught on something. At first he thought it was a small root from the new growth at the base of one of the cottonwoods.

But as he reached down to free his boot, he saw that it wasn't a root but a leather strap protruding from the dirt. It was attached to something buried under one of the exposed roots.

He pulled on the strap and a small leather shoulder bag came up out of the dirt. The leather was discolored, the design faded over the years, but he recognized it at once.

His heart pounded against his injured ribs. Jessica's purse.

Chapter Two

Emma had just put the pies in the oven when the phone rang. She stared at it a moment, not sure she wanted to answer it after the last time.

"You want me to get that?" the cook asked. Celeste was a thirty-something woman, robust, flush-faced and tireless. What she lacked in a sense of humor was made up by her work ethic. At least that's what Emma told herself.

"No, I have it." Emma wiped her hands on her apron and walked to the wall phone in the kitchen. She picked it up on the third ring, praying it wasn't a repeat of the two other calls she'd gotten since arriving here.

"Chisholm Cattle Company," she said into the phone.

A beat of silence, then, "Mrs. Hoyt Chisholm?" The voice was a woman's. She sounded elderly and according to the caller ID, a local number.

"Yes." Emma held her breath, hoping the woman was someone from the nearby town of Whitehorse who'd called to welcome her to the area and wish her well on her marriage.

"You need to get out of that house before you end up dead, too. Your husband is cursed when it comes to wives."

"I'm sorry, but what are you talking about?" Emma asked.

"The Chisholm curse. You've been warned." As the woman slammed down the phone, Emma jerked the receiver away from her ear.

"Something wrong?" Celeste asked.

"Wrong number." She hung up hoping the cook didn't see the way her hand was shaking. Emma wasn't ready to confide in either Celeste or the housekeeper, Mae. She'd seen how shocked they'd been that Hoyt had remarried. While neither of them had said anything, she'd noticed that they stayed to themselves, rebuffing any attempts she made to gain their trust—let alone their friendship.

"How long have you worked for Mr. Chisholm?" Emma asked Celeste now. She hadn't want to ask too many questions, hoping to gain the employees' trust by being helpful and pleasant and find out more about each of the women—and more about Whitehorse and how

Chisholm Cattle Company fit into the scheme of things—as time went on.

That, she'd come to realize, wasn't going to happen.

"Just over a year," Celeste said.

"And Mae?"

"About six months."

Emma felt her brow shoot up in surprise.

"Not a lot of people want to work out here," Celeste said.

"Why is that?" She knew the wages were good and Hoyt was congenial and easy to work for, from what she'd seen.

The cook seemed to search her gaze, as if she wondered if Emma was joking. Or testing her. "It's a long drive."

She could tell there was more, but that the woman wasn't going to tell her for some reason. "Surely *someone* lasted longer."

Celeste shook her head. "Not that I know of."

Emma wondered if it had anything to do with the Chisholm Curse. She hated to admit that the phone calls had shaken her a little.

"Those women who have been calling you, they're just jealous," her friend Debra had said when she called Denver later that afternoon. Celeste had left for the day and it was Mae's day off. Emma had the house to herself until supper when Celeste would return to help her cook for her large new family.

"Hoyt Chisholm must have been the most eligible bachelor in all of Montana," her friend said. "Don't let some old biddies get to you. He picked *you*. He loves *you*."

Yes, Emma thought. And she loved Hoyt. "Still, it seems odd." The last elderly neighboring ranchwoman's call hadn't sounded malicious. She'd sounded scared for her.

COLTON WAS WAITING BY THE ROAD when he finally saw the Sheriff's Department patrol car approaching. His mind was reeling from the letter—and what he'd found under the cottonwood tree.

Inside Jessica's purse he'd discovered her wallet with her driver's license, $200 in cash and a bus ticket out of Whitehorse.

One one-way bus ticket? She'd said she wanted them to run away together. While she didn't have a car of her own, she knew he had his own pickup. Did she have so little faith that he would show up that she'd gotten the ticket just in case? He felt confused. The ticket had been for the 4:00 a.m. bus that would have left just hours after they were to meet at their secret spot.

Why had she thought she'd be leaving Whitehorse alone?

But if her purse was buried under the tree root, then how could she have left town? And why would she bury her purse? It made no sense. It made his blood run cold because he know she wouldn't have buried it—just as he couldn't see how she could have left without it.

A terrible dread had settled into his bones by the time the sheriff's deputy pulled up next to his pickup and a female deputy stepped out.

She wore jeans, cowboy boots and a tan uniform shirt with a Whitehorse County Sheriff's Department patch on the sleeve. Colton felt his heart drop like a stone off a cliff as he recognized her. He swore under his breath. Just when he thought things couldn't get any worse. *"Halley?"*

DEPUTY HALLEY ROBINSON had told herself after moving back to Whitehorse that sooner or later she was going to cross paths with Colton Chisholm. When she'd left Whitehorse after junior high school, hadn't she sworn that one day she would return and make Colton sorry?

But that had been a young girl's dream of revenge. Halley was no longer that young, impressionable girl. Lucky for Colton, she thought, since here they both were again, and oh, how the tables had turned.

"Colton," she said, secretly enjoying the fact that he'd remembered her.

"*You're* the new deputy?"

She smiled in answer. When the call came in, she'd been the only one on duty in the area. The county was a large one, stretching from the Missouri River to the south and all the way to Canada on the north.

"So, why don't you tell me what the problem is," she said, all business again. "You told the dispatcher you'd found Jessica Granger's purse and you believe something might have happened to her?"

He nodded, looking as if he now regretted making that call to the sheriff's office. Reaching into the cab of his pickup, he lifted out a weathered leather purse and handed it to her.

"It's Jessica's. I found it at a spot we used to meet."

She raised her gaze to his. "A *secret* spot, the dispatcher said."

He chewed at the inside of his cheek for a moment. "That's right."

"And there was something about a lost letter?"

Colton rubbed the back of his neck. His hair

was longer than she'd ever seen it, but back in junior high, his father had taken clippers to all six of the boys, giving them buzz cuts. That was probably why she hadn't remembered the color, a combination of ripe wheat and sunshine that brought out the gold flecks in his blue eyes.

She felt that old quiver inside as her gaze me his. Colton Chisholm had been adorable in grade school. It shouldn't have surprised her that he'd grown into a drop-dead good-looking man.

He reached into his jean jacket pocket and brought out a worse-for-wear looking, age-yellowed envelope. He held it as if not wanting to relinquish the letter to her, then finally handed it over.

Halley noted the postmark and the return address before opening the envelope. She quickly read what Jessica had written on the single sheet inside. The writing was young, girlish. She remembered Jessica Granger only too well. Jessica had been one of those annoyingly silly, all-girl girls while Halley had been a daredevil, tree-climbing, ball-throwing, horse-riding tomboy.

The letter, she noted, had been mailed fourteen years ago—only a few years after Halley had left Whitehorse brokenhearted because of Colton Chisholm.

Her gaze slid up to his again. He looked damn uncomfortable. Guilt? "What was it she had to tell you?"

He shook his head. "I didn't get the letter until today."

"You're saying you didn't meet her that night?"

"No. How could I since I never got the *letter?*" He sounded both angry and upset and she could see that he was more than a little shaken by this. He turned to get a United States Postal Department manila envelope from the pickup cab. He thrust it at her. "You can check with Albert if you don't believe me."

Halley wasn't sure what she believed. She was having a hard time separating the boy he'd been from the man standing before her. As a boy, he'd been too cute for his own good. Now he had a rough, sexy look about him that was enhanced by what was clearly a strong, worked-hard, ranch body.

She was sure women found him irresistible and wondered how many hearts he'd broken. It made her think of her own fragile, small one that had taken a beating all those years ago because of him.

"Jessica didn't phone you when you didn't show up? Didn't try to contact you?"

His golden gaze met hers and held it. "I never saw her again. I was told that she left town, just like she said she was going to do in the letter. I tried to find out where she'd gone, but…" He wagged his head and looked down at the toes of his Western boots. "Her family wouldn't tell me anything. Her dad didn't like me."

Imagine that. "You have a fight?"

He looked away toward the foothills, his face filled with a pain that could have been guilt. Or she supposed it was possible he'd really cared about this girl. It amazed her that the thought could still hurt.

"It was just a stupid disagreement," he said finally.

"Over…?"

"Nothing, just dumb high school stuff."

He was lying. Halley wondered what the fight had been about and whom he was trying to protect. Jessica Granger? Or himself? Jessica had said in the letter she wanted to tell him something that night.

"Would you have gone away with her?"

He swung his gaze back to her as if surprised by the question. "I was in love with her. I would have done anything she asked."

Halley nodded, unable to hide her surprise by his impassioned response—or her quick flash of jealousy. There'd been a time she would have given anything to have the boy Colton had been feel that way about *her*.

"Why do I get the feeling there is a whole lot more to this?" Maybe she just wanted to believe it because this was Colton Chisholm she was dealing with.

He didn't answer. The look he gave her said he feared she was incapable of believing anything he told her. He could be right about that. Clearly, she wasn't the only one who remembered their history. Call it puppy love, kid stuff, whatever, those old hurts lasted a lifetime.

"Why a letter? Why didn't she just call you and ask you to meet her?"

Colton hung his head, studying his boot toes again. "I don't know. Maybe her father wouldn't let her call."

"Or maybe she thought you wouldn't take her call."

He shot her an angry look. "We had an argument. Her dad didn't want her seeing me. It was complicated. None of that has anything to do with anything."

Halley lifted a brow, unconvinced.

"Look, I don't care what you think about me, I just need to know what happened to her."

"What do you *think* happened to her?"

Colton shifted, anger making his broad shoulders appear even broader. He looked ready to take her on, just as he had when they were kids. Except that he appeared to have already been in a fight. He was favoring his ribs and there was discoloration around one of his eyes. This time it hadn't been some skinny, spunky tomboy in the school yard who'd given him the shiner, though, she suspected.

"Let's cut to the chase," he said, a muscle tightening in his jaw. "Jessica wouldn't have left without her purse that night."

"So you think she's still out there," Halley said and felt a chill snake up her spine. "I think you'd better show me this secret place of yours and I'm going to have to keep this letter—at least until we get this cleared up."

COLTON DIDN'T WANT TO come back to the spot on the creek. It had been tough enough earlier. Now it was pure hell. He felt sick to his stomach as Halley parked the patrol SUV in the clearing and cut the engine. She'd insisted that he ride with her. He could feel her watching him, looking for…what? Proof that he was everything she thought he was and worse?

Hell, he'd never felt more guilty in his life. He'd let Jessica down. Hadn't been there for her when she'd needed him the most. Because in his heart, he knew what they were going to find here. In his heart, he knew Jessica had never left their secret spot that night.

The sun pounded down with a heat that stole his breath. The quiet was deafening as they climbed out of the SUV and walked along the secluded path toward the stand of cottonwoods. It was as if every living thing had deserted the area. Even the water in the small creek fell silent.

"This is where I found the purse," he said when they finally reached the grove of trees. "I tripped on the strap." He could feel her gaze on him before she glanced around. He could imagine what she was thinking. He felt anger rise in him again, but swallowed it back. "I didn't kill her."

Halley's brow quirked up. "You're that sure she's dead?"

"Can we please stop playing games here? We both know she's dead. She wouldn't have left without her purse and she damn sure didn't bury it herself under that tree root." His voice broke. "You have to find her so she can get a proper burial."

"Where would you suggest we look for a body?" the deputy asked, clearly baiting him.

"Do you have any idea how hard this is on

me?" he asked through clenched teeth. He had taken a step toward her, but now stopped, suddenly aware that her hand was resting on the butt of her gun. Did she really think he'd killed Jessica?

The heat, the quiet, the sickness in the pit of his stomach made him slump down on the edge of the creek bank. He put his head in his hands and fought back all the emotions warring inside him. "Please, just find her."

HALLEY PULLED OUT her cell phone, all the while keeping an eye on Colton. He hadn't moved from the creek bank. She got the number for Sid and Mildred Granger's house. A woman picked up on the third ring.

"I'd like to speak with Jessica Granger," Halley said and saw Colton lift his head. He frowned, the look he gave her appeared to question whether she'd lost her mind.

There was a beat of silence, then, "She isn't here. She doesn't live here anymore."

"Can you tell me where I can reach her?"

Another beat of silence. "May I ask who's calling?"

"Is this Mrs. Granger?"

"Yes."

Halley heard the hesitation in the woman's voice. "I'm Sheriff's Deputy Halley Robinson.

I know this is unusual, but can you tell me when you last heard from your daughter?"

"A week ago. We got a letter. Has something happened to her?" The woman sounded scared.

"No, I'm sorry to upset you. But I would like to stop by and ask you a few questions. Something of your daughter's has been found. I'd like to return it."

"Something of Jessica's?"

"I'll come by now if that's all right. Is your husband home as well?"

"Yes, but—"

"I'll see you shortly." She snapped the phone shut and looked at Colton. "I talked to Jessica's mother. She says she got a letter from Jessica just last week. I'm going over there now to—"

"I'm going with you," Colton said, shooting to his feet. "She's lying. Jessica couldn't have written her last week."

A shaft of ice ran up her spine, even though the heat at the edge of the cottonwoods was intense. Why was he was so adamant that Jessica was dead unless…he'd killed her? She suddenly felt the isolation of this secret place where he used to meet his girlfriend. It wouldn't be the first time she'd stood face-to-face with a killer. But it would be the first time it was a killer she'd once loved.

"Why would her mother lie?" Halley managed to ask.

"I don't know, but she's lying. If Jessica was alive…" His voice trailed off, anguish twisted his handsome features into a mask of pain. "I want to see the letter she supposedly sent last week. I knew Jessica better than anyone."

Was that so? She had no doubt that Colton had known Jessica intimately if this secret spot under the cottonwoods was any indication. But if he'd known her so well, then why didn't he know what Jessica couldn't wait to tell him that night?

One thing was clear. Colton was going to the Granger house. Better he go with her.

"Okay, you can come with me. But if you cause any trouble, you'll be leaving their house in handcuffs, understood?"

He nodded and she couldn't help but notice how pale he looked. She'd never seen Colton Chisholm this vulnerable. She'd thought it would give her some satisfaction. It didn't.

EMMA FOUND HER HUSBAND in the barn. He hadn't gone to move cattle with all of his sons except for Colton, which wasn't like him. She worried that he wasn't feeling well. Or that something was bothering him. Probably her. Maybe he was regretting his impulsive rush to the altar.

She'd noticed that he'd been spending more time in the barn with his horses lately. Apparently, this is where he went when he was upset about something. She stopped just inside the door to watch him as he curried a palomino mare. Hoyt was in his late fifties, just a few years older than she was. He was a big, physically fit man with a thick head of blond hair that made the gray in it hardly noticeable. But what had stolen her heart like a thief was his penetrating blue eyes and self-deprecating charm.

She wondered about the other women who'd passed through his life and this curse her latest caller had mentioned. Had those women only known the Hoyt who laughed a lot and lived hard? Or had they stuck around long enough to know this Hoyt, the quiet, gentle rancher who Emma loved and worried about?

At breakfast she'd noticed that he was quieter than usual. Now she was sure something was eating at him and wondered how long it would take before he confided in her. Or if he would.

She was sure the other women who'd been in his life had been younger, slimmer and no doubt more beautiful than she was. She couldn't help but wonder what had made him fall in love with her.

But whatever those other women had been like, Emma didn't think Hoyt realized yet that he had a woman strong enough that he could lean on her.

He turned as if sensing her presence. His face lit up at the sight of her and sent her heart racing and her pulse drumming in her ears. It amazed her that this man had the ability to do that to her. She didn't doubt that Hoyt Chisholm would be able to fill her with this same desire when she was ninety.

"Coming out here will only get you in trouble," Hoyt said as he reached for her. He pulled her to him, nuzzled her neck, making her skin tingle. She felt his fingers slip under her Western shirt and skim across her bare midriff.

As he drew back, his gaze met hers, desire burning like a hot, blue flame.

"Have you ever made love in a hayloft?" he whispered as he leaned in to kiss her.

"Never," she whispered back when she was able to catch her breath. Clearly he had something else in mind other than talking about what was really bothering him. If he thought he could distract her… Well, he was right.

"But you've secretly wanted to, haven't

you?" He was grinning at her and she knew she would have given him anything.

"How is it you always seem to know my secret desires, Hoyt Chisholm?"

Without another word he took her hand and led her through the barn to the foot of the hay-loft ladder. "Ladies first."

She saw the dare in his gaze and had a feeling no other woman had been up this ladder with him. Emma kissed him and began to climb.

"WHAT THE HELL is *he* doing here?"

Halley studied the man standing framed in the Granger house doorway. She vaguely remembered Sid Granger. She'd seen him around town when she was a girl because he'd worked for the city and probably still did.

"I need to speak with you and your wife," Halley said flashing her badge. It had little effect on Sid, though. He stood glaring at Colton, looking as if he wanted to kill him. "Mr. Granger, I have something of your daughter Jessica's."

She held up the purse, finally getting his attention.

"That's not my daughter's."

"It has Jessica's driver's license in it. I believe it *is* her purse." Behind him a small woman appeared in a housedress and long apron, the quintessential homemaker. Millie Granger? When the woman's eyes lit on the purse, her expression changed instantly. Suddenly she looked worried.

"Why don't you ask your wife if it's Jessica's purse," Halley said.

"It's Jessica's," Millie said in a small voice. "Let them come in."

Sid seemed surprised, but stepped back.

Halley shot Colton a look and said under her breath, "What did you do to make him hate you so much?"

Colton shook his head. "The son of a bitch was crazy when it came to Jessica."

They followed the Grangers inside the house.

The interior of the house came as a surprise. Given the way Millie Granger was dressed, Halley had expected a lot of doilies, ruffled curtains and crocheted pillows. Instead, the feel was more masculine, including the huge stretched and dried rattlesnake skin that hung over the fireplace. She shivered. She'd never liked snakes, but she shouldn't have been that surprised that Sid Granger did.

Sid turned abruptly the moment they were inside. "I don't want him in my hou—"

"Colton found your daughter's purse," Halley

said, raising her voice over his. "As I said, her driver's license is in it along with a bus ticket from fourteen years ago and $200 in cash."

Sid shook his head. "How is that possible?"

"That's what we'd like to know. Did your daughter mention losing her purse?" she asked the mother.

Millie was a petite woman who looked as if she might blow away in a strong wind. The word *mousy* came to mind and, Halley noticed, Millie Granger was also clearly nervous. She was wearing a faded print apron. She kneaded the hem of it in her fingers, worrying at a hole in the fabric as she looked at her husband, as if fearful of what he might do.

Halley was wondering the same thing. Sid Granger's jaw was set, his body practically trembling with anger.

"There must be some mistake," Millie said in a small voice, her gaze still on her husband.

"You say you heard from your daughter last week?" Halley asked. Neither answered. "Is there a problem?" Clearly, there was, since Millie seemed to be waiting for her husband to say something.

"It's a family matter," Sid said through clenched teeth. "We don't discuss family matters with—"

"She ran away fourteen years ago," Millie blurted out, finally dragging her gaze from her husband. Sid shot her a lethal look.

Halley already knew from the letter Colton had received that running away had been Jessica's plan. "Was there an argument?"

Sid Granger had his lips clamped shut. He was still glaring at his wife.

"We didn't hear from her for a while," Millie said timidly. "But then we got a letter from her."

"So you've been in contact with her?" Halley asked. Again the Grangers exchanged a look. "You've *talked* to her?"

"She writes every year on her birthday, but there is never a return address and she mails the letters from different places. She doesn't want us to know where she is." Millie's voice broke.

"It's not us she is trying to get away from," Sid bellowed. "It's *him!*" He thrust a finger at Colton. "We lost our daughter because of him!" He took a menacing step toward him. "I want this man out of my house. *Now.*"

"Let's all settle down," Halley said, giving Colton a warning look as she stepped between the two men.

"Jessica got away from him and I won't have him—"

"You're the reason she was leaving," Colton snapped. "She would have done anything to get out of this house and away from you."

"Maybe it would be better if *you* left," Halley said, turning to glare at Colton. He was only making the situation worse.

"I'm not going anywhere until I see the letter from Jessica."

Halley would have liked to haul him out of the house in handcuffs just as she'd warned him. "If we could all just calm down."

"Not until that bastard is out of my house!"

"Sid, let the deputy tell us why she's here," Millie Granger said loudly, then quickly lowered her voice. "Please." She kneaded again at the tear in her apron, her voice again as tiny as she was.

The tension in the room dropped a notch.

"Could we all sit down?" Halley asked.

Sid grudgingly took a chair, scowling the whole time at Colton, who sat down on one end of the couch, Halley on the other. She wondered what he'd done to Jessica that warranted this much hatred from the girl's father. Was Colton right and it was just a father's love of his only daughter? Or something more sinister on either of the two men's parts?

"We need to be sure that Jessica is all right,"

Halley said. "Finding her purse raises questions, as I'm sure you realize. Could I see the letters from your daughter?"

This time Millie didn't look to her husband for guidance. She rose and, avoiding his gaze, went to a bedroom off the living room. She returned a few moments later with a small bundle of letters tied with a red ribbon.

She handed them to the deputy. As Halley undid the ribbon, she noted that there were over a dozen letters.

Before she could react, Colton stood and leaned over to snatch the top envelope from the pile.

Sid Granger shot out of his chair. Halley quickly took the letter back. But not before Colton had let out a cry that sounded almost like a sob.

"That isn't Jessica's handwriting," he said, his voice breaking, as he snatched another envelope from her hand, opened it and pulled out the short letter. He looked devastated. "These letters aren't from Jessica."

Chapter Three

Colton felt as if he'd been kicked in the chest by a mule. All these years her parents had believed she was alive because of letters that weren't from her at all?

"How could you believe the letters were from Jessica?" he demanded.

Millie was crying and wringing her hands in the cloth of her apron. Her husband looked as if he was trying to restrain himself. Colton was glad he hadn't opted to come here without the deputy because he was having the same problem not going for Sid Granger's throat.

"A person's handwriting can change," Millie was saying through her tears.

"If she was alive, why wouldn't she *call?*" Colton demanded. "Why was Jessica so afraid to let her own family know where she was unless she hated you so much—"

"You punk!" Sid Granger sprang to his feet. "It was you she was trying to get away from."

"Why would Jessica send me a letter asking me to run away with her if I was the problem?" Colton demanded, not backing down as he, too, shot to his feet.

"Colton," the deputy warned as she stepped between them again. "Mr. Granger, I need to know why you're so angry at Mr. Chisholm."

Colton narrowed his gaze at her. Clearly, she was looking for just one more reason to hang him, but he stepped back, raising his hands in surrender.

"What was it you thought Mr. Chisholm did to your daughter?" Halley asked again.

Sid Granger seemed to have trouble speaking. He swallowed several times, his Adam's apple bobbing up and down. Tears filled his eyes. He hastily brushed them away with his shirtsleeve. Anger reddened his face. He opened his mouth, but nothing came out.

"He got her pregnant," Millie said from the rocker where she'd been sitting crying.

Colton took the news like a blow. He lowered himself to the couch. Looking up, he saw the deputy's face. She'd obviously been anticipating something like this. Was this the news Jessica had wanted to tell him that night?

"He knocked her up and refused to marry her," Sid finally managed to get out.

"No!" Colton bellowed. "That's a lie. I didn't

know. She never…" His voice broke with emotion as it sank in. "I didn't know," he said more to himself than to the people in the room. He could feel Halley's gaze on him. He doubted she believed him any more than Sid Granger did.

"As Mr. Chisholm said, your daughter wrote him a letter before the night she was to leave," the deputy was saying. "That letter was lost and only delivered today. In the letter, she said she wanted him to run away with her. Do you know if she met him that night?"

"Why don't you ask him?" Sid snapped. "He's sitting right there."

"I'm asking you. When was the last time you saw your daughter?"

Millie spoke up from where the rocker. "I saw her that afternoon. She said she needed to run an errand. I wouldn't let her take the car so she had her friend Twyla pick her up."

"Twyla?" Halley asked.

"Twyla Reynolds." Millie looked to Sid. He had sat back down again and now had one arm over his face. "Sid, when was the last time *you* saw Jessica?"

"That evening after she came home," he said, his words muffled. "She said she was going to bed. I just assumed…"

"You have to understand," Millie said. "The

letters… We wanted to believe that she was alive. If I noticed something different about the way she wrote, I just thought it was because she'd changed over the years."

"Didn't you ever wonder what she'd done with the baby?" Colton asked, still angry because something had been wrong in this house or Jessica would never have been at their secret spot that night. She would never have needed to run away. She would still be alive today.

He could see that Deputy Halley Robinson was asking questions as if she still thought Jessica might be alive. She was the only person in this room, though, who believed that now.

"I'd hoped that she had the baby and was raising our grandchild…" Millie looked away.

"I'd like to have a handwriting expert look at the letters that were sent to you," Halley said. "If you get any more, please try not to handle them so we can dust them for prints."

Millie nodded distractedly. "We weren't due to get another one for almost a year. I would imagine they will stop coming now."

Only if the killer finds out that Jessica's disappearance is being investigated, Colton thought. But the way news spread in this county, if the killer was still around, he would know soon enough.

"Do you have anything Jessica wrote before she left that we could compare it to?" Halley was asking.

Millie pushed herself to her feet. "I'm sure there is something in her room. It's just as she left it."

Colton started to rise to follow the deputy and Millie upstairs to Jessica's room, but Sid Granger stopped him.

"You aren't going in her room," Sid said, blocking his way. "If you hadn't gotten her pregnant…"

"Why don't you wait outside," Halley suggested to Colton.

He could have put up a fight, but he didn't have any fight left in him and there was nothing more to accomplish in this house, even if he could stand another moment in it. All he could think about was Jessica. She had been pregnant with his baby. But they'd been so careful. Not that any of that mattered now.

She must have been planning to tell him about the baby that night. Hadn't she realized that he would have been excited about the prospect of being a father? He would never have deserted her. Never.

As he left the house, he tried to swallow the lump in his throat at the realization that if he was right and Jessica had never left the spot under the trees that night, then his baby had died with her.

"I think I have everything I need for now," Halley said a few moments later as she and Millie came out through the screen door to the porch and started down the steps to where Colton was waiting.

As she headed for her patrol SUV parked in the yard, she shot him a look. He could tell that she'd found more of Jessica's handwriting and it matched the letter he'd received fourteen years too late—not the ones someone had been sending her parents in the interim.

"I'll let you know what we find out," the deputy promised Millie who'd followed them as far as the vehicle and stood looking even smaller and even more terrified.

Colton saw her glance back toward the house. Sid stood in the doorway. Millie Granger visibly shuddered at the sight of her husband. As Colton looked toward the man in the doorway, he thought of the man's temper, his obsession with Jessica, his hatred of Colton. What if Sid had followed his daughter that night and caught her at the secret spot on the creek?

"You all right?" the deputy asked as she started the SUV.

He could feel her gaze on him as he suppressed a chill at the thought of what Sid

Granger might have been capable of when it came to his daughter—was still capable of doing when it came to his wife.

"You didn't know she was pregnant."

It wasn't a question but he answered anyway. "No."

"I assume the baby was yours?"

He looked over at her, anger hitting him again with sudden heat. "Why would you even ask that? You saw the letter. She wanted me to run away with her."

Halley nodded, but said nothing until they were back at his pickup parked at the edge of the road where he'd left it earlier. As he started to get out of the patrol car, she said, "I'm going to need a sample of your handwriting."

EMMA WOULD HAVE SAID she was the luckiest woman in the world if anyone had asked her just three seconds ago.

Moments before she'd been lying on the soft warm blanket on the pile of hay beside her husband, his arm around her, trying to catch her breath after their lovemaking. She'd been wondering if other people their age still felt like this, and felt bad for them if they didn't.

But then Hoyt's cell phone had vibrated on the blanket beside him and he'd snatched it up, checked to see who was calling, then he'd seemed to hesitate as if wanting to take the call and yet—

"Go ahead," Emma had said, sitting up to stretch. She knew how he was about business. Running this ranch was what kept him young.

"I really need to take this." He rose stark naked and walked down to the end of the hayloft.

Any other time Emma wouldn't have paid any attention, but something in the way Hoyt was standing, his back to her, his shoulders slumped over slightly, his voice low…

Her heart suddenly took off at a gallop as she noticed something that hadn't fully registered before. This wasn't the first time he'd checked to see who was calling and said, "I need to take this," and hurried out of the room. Or taken the call out on the porch. Or rushed downstairs. Or, like now, moved to the other end of the hayloft. These calls weren't about ranch business.

Ice-cold fear moved through her. She couldn't hear what he was saying but she could read his body language. There was secrecy in the way he spoke into the phone.

Emma tried to fight the terror that clutched her heart like a fist. She told herself that she was being foolish. Hoyt loved her. Only her. She had no reason to question his love.

He snapped the phone shut, turned toward her and she saw his face and knew. Her husband looked guilty as hell.

Emma had never thought she'd be one of those women who didn't want to know the truth. But right now, she felt too vulnerable, lying naked on a horse blanket in a hayloft after making love to the man she loved.

Quickly she hid her own face so he couldn't see her fear as she reached for her clothes.

HALLEY CALLED SHERIFF McCall Crawford, who was in Great Falls tied up on a federal case, to update her on the Granger case.

"Sheriff Winchester, I mean, Crawford," McCall said with a small laugh.

The sheriff wasn't the only one who was having trouble getting used to her married name. Most everyone in town still referred to her as Sheriff Winchester. When Halley filled the sheriff in, McCall told her to let the state crime investigators take the case from here on out—and to wait for their arrival.

When the team arrived by small plane that afternoon, she drove them to the crime scene, which a deputy had cordoned off, and waited to make sure nothing was disturbed.

Earlier, she'd told Colton to go home, warning him not to leave town.

He'd actually pulled himself together enough to chuckle at that on the drive back to his pickup from the Granger house.

"You must think I'm an idiot. You probably already suspect I'm a murderer. But do you really think I'm going to make a run for it?"

"I don't know, are you?" He'd given her an impatient look and she'd had to ask, "So tell me about Jessica."

"What do you want to know?" He'd sounded despondent.

"What was she like?" Halley remembered Jessica Granger, the girl Colton had started chasing at the end of junior high. Shortly after that Halley had talked her father into moving away from Whitehorse. "You were in love with her, right? There must have been a reason."

He had looked out the side window for so long she'd thought he wasn't going to answer. "You're not going to understand because she wasn't like you."

She'd shot him a look, not sure how to take that, but taking it badly, just the same.

"Jessica wasn't strong. She needed me."

"*That* was the appeal?" Halley asked in surprise.

He had finally looked in her direction.

"Jessica needed someone to take care of her, to protect her from her old man. But I failed her."

"She needed protection from her father?" Halley couldn't help thinking about how she herself had needed someone to protect her from Colton Chisholm. She'd had to learn to fight her own battles. No one had come to her rescue. The thought drove the arrow even deeper in her heart and made her all the more angry that Colton, when he'd finally fallen for a girl, had fallen for one who he said himself was nothing like her.

"You met Sid," was all he said before climbing out of the patrol car.

She'd watched him go, seeing the toll this was taking on him, telling herself that a murderer might act the same way, especially if he couldn't take the guilt anymore.

Now, as Halley watched the crime techs begin the search for a body, she told herself her suspicions about Colton had nothing to do with how she felt about him today or all those years ago when he'd broken her tender heart.

The breeze stirred the cottonwoods as the creek whispered past. It seemed too beautiful a spot for the crime techs to be looking for a young woman's remains, but there was little doubt in her mind now that Jessica Granger was dead, that she'd died here.

Whether or not they would find Jessica, though, was another story. Halley suspected it would have been a shallow grave somewhere along this creek bottom. Which meant animals could have dug up the grave and carried away the bones years ago.

"I MIGHT NEED A LAWYER."

Emma had been picking at her supper but looked up now as everyone else at the table turned toward Colton. Like her, he'd hardly touched his food and he'd passed on apple pie. That wasn't like him. Hoyt hadn't eaten much, either. There was almost a full piece of pie on his plate.

"A lawyer?" she repeated. Since Hoyt's call in the barn, she'd tried to keep busy and think about anything but her own horrible suspicions.

"Why would you need a lawyer?" Hoyt asked.

Colton rubbed a hand over his jaw. "To make a long story short, there's at least one law enforcement officer in the county who thinks I killed Jessica Granger."

Hoyt froze, fork in hand. "*What?* I thought she left town."

Emma noticed that her husband had gone very pale.

"Apparently, she planned on leaving but I don't think she made it. Neither does the deputy now scouring a spot not far from here for her remains," Colton said, pain in his voice.

"I don't understand why they would think someone killed her," Hoyt said and Emma found herself studying her husband. Of course he'd be upset about such an allegation against his son, but when he set down his fork, she saw that his hand was shaking.

A bad feeling lodged itself in her chest as Colton proceeded to tell them about a lost letter, finding Jessica's purse buried under a tree root and calling the Sheriff's Department.

"Halley Robinson?" his brother, Tanner, asked with a smirk. "Isn't that the girl that you used to—"

"She's the new deputy," Colton said, shooting his brother a warning look.

Emma waited for Hoyt to jump in. When he didn't, she felt as if her world had suddenly shifted on its axis and nothing was as it had been just hours before.

"Isn't it possible the girl isn't even dead? They haven't found anything yet, right?" she asked.

Colton shook his head. "She wouldn't have left without her purse."

"What does the sheriff have to say about this?" Hoyt asked.

"From what I've been able to find out, the *sheriff* is busy in federal court on another case. This one has been turned over to the state crime team, but a fourteen-year-old possible murder isn't going to be at the top of their list of investigations. Even if the sheriff was in town, I'm not sure it would keep Halley from trying to railroad me."

"Well, you're just going to have to change this Halley person's mind," Emma said and saw her husband give her a sympathetic smile at her naiveté.

"Emma's is one approach," Hoyt said. "We'll also get you the best lawyer money can buy, just in case you can't convince this woman that you're innocent. I take it the two of you have some kind of history?"

"You could say that," Tanner said.

His other brothers had been feeding their faces, but now joined in. "Wait a minute," Zane said. "That's not that little dark-haired skinny girl—"

"She isn't so little anymore," Dawson said, laughing. "I saw her but didn't realize she was

Halley Robinson. She's gorgeous." He let out a whistle.

Emma could see that Colton was at the end of his rope as Logan and Marshall chimed in with similar remarks.

"Let's take our dishes into the kitchen and let your father and Colton talk about this alone," she suggested, then stood and gave them each a look that sent the bunch of them quickly to their feet.

Colton shot her a thankful glance as she marched them all to the kitchen and closed the door behind them.

"Okay," she said once they were out of hearing range. "Tell me about this Halley Robinson."

HALLEY FOUND HER FATHER out in the south forty. He looked up as she came riding in. His face crinkled into a smile at the sight of her and she knew she'd made the right decision coming back to Whitehorse, Montana, with him.

He'd missed ranching and she knew the only reason he'd left here was because she'd been so unhappy. They were the only family they had.

"Hey, didn't expect to see you so soon," Geoff Robinson said as he finished tightening the top strand of barbed wire, then pulled off his gloves and turned all his attention to his daughter. "Everything all right?"

"I tried to call you on your cell," she said, swinging down from her horse.

"Oh, hell," he said feeling in his pocket. He grinned, "Guess I forgot it on the kitchen table. Sorry."

"It's all right. I needed the ride anyway." She'd been worried about him when she couldn't reach him and hadn't even thought to check to see if he'd taken his cell phone. He hated the damn thing and said one of the reasons he'd wanted to come back to Whitehorse was so he didn't have to carry it.

Still it worried her, him being out here alone, even though she could see how happy he was working on this old place.

"Should be able to get some cattle soon," he said now, smiling at her. "Just a big enough herd to make a little profit and keep us fed." His smile fell. "Rough day?"

"Had to go out to the Chisholm place," she said.

"Chisholm, huh."

"Colton Chisholm called the Sheriff's Department because he found his former girlfriend's purse buried in a spot the two of them used to meet fourteen years ago. There's a crime tech team searching for her remains as we speak."

"Is that right?"

She shot him a warning look.

"Sorry," he said, holding up his hands. "I know that boy drove you crazy but you held your own and quite frankly, I think—"

"I know what you thought," she said, cutting him off. Her father had told her she had to learn to fight her own battles. And she had. She knew he believed it had made her stronger, being raised like a son instead of a daughter.

But then he'd also thought that Colton Chisholm was just trying to get her attention all those years ago. Well, he certainly had her attention now.

Chapter Four

"I don't understand," Emma said after listening to her stepsons tell her about Halley Robinson. "Why would this woman have it in for Colton if all he did was have a crush on her?"

"He acted stupid around her," Tanner said. "Did stupid things like chase her with a frog and put gross things down her neck and knock her down in the school yard."

Emma sighed. She feared Colton was no better with women now than he'd been back in grade school with Halley Robinson.

"The funny part was that she always fought back and usually Colton got the worst of it, although he didn't let her know it," Dawson said, laughing. "Blackened his eye one time and almost broke his arm another. I'm sure Colton is the reason the Robinson family moved away. He just wouldn't leave her alone. That was until one day when he had to rescue Jessica from some bully."

Emma sighed more deeply. This was looking worse all the time. "What else do you know about Halley Robinson?"

Her stepsons shrugged. "She used to be this cute little dark-haired girl with big brown eyes and now she's beautiful," Dawson said.

"She was too mean to be cute. She really did have it in for Colton before her family left town," Marshall said. "If she's now a deputy and she thinks Colton murdered his old girlfriend, who knows what she'll do to see that he hangs for it."

"They don't hang killers in Montana anymore," Dawson said. "But they could send him to the chair."

"Your brother isn't going to any chair," Emma snapped and her stepsons scattered like geese out the back door and across the lawn. She watched them go, her heart in her throat as she wondered about Colton's relationship with Jessica Granger.

That was the problem with being dropped in the middle of these strangers' lives. She knew nothing about her stepsons. She didn't even know her husband, as it was turning out. Just the thought of Hoyt sent another arrow to pierce her already wounded heart.

Love conquered all, right? Or broke your heart, she reminded herself remembering the

look on Colton's face. Jessica Granger, whoever she had been, had broken his.

Celeste came into the kitchen with the last
of the dishes. Emma fell in beside her to help,
even though the young woman assured her it
wasn't necessary. It was her house now. She
could do dishes if she dang well pleased

GEOFF ROBINSON COULD SEE THAT Halley
didn't want to hear what he had to say about
Colton Chisholm so he just shut his mouth
and studied his daughter. She was the spitting
image of her mother, Mary Lou, rest her soul.
A beauty with a fire that would take a special
man to appreciate.

He thought of the boy who used to follow
Halley home from school, a gangly, towheaded
Chisholm kid he'd heard had grown into a
good man, a hardworking rancher and a good-
looking cowboy.

Halley had always thought Colton Chisholm
was a royal pain in the neck, but Geoff had
seen something in the boy that told him the
kid was all right—if a little misguided.

"You can't believe how he torments me," she
used to complain.

"It's because he likes you."

She'd been so flabbergasted that she hadn't
even been able to speak for a few moments.

"He put a frog down my neck. Does that sound like he likes me?"

"It's what boys at that age do if they like a girl."

"I blackened his eye," she said, looking proud of the fact.

"Halley!"

"I told him I would break his arm if he pulled something like that again."

He'd realized then that Mary Lou would have been horrified to see the way he'd raised their precious daughter. But it wasn't until later that Geoff realized what he'd done.

Suddenly, the Chisholm boy was no longer tailing after Halley on the dirt road. Geoff had seen how miserable his little girl became, but he hadn't completely understood it until he found her crying on the porch one night not long after that. He asked her what was wrong even though he suspected he knew.

"Colton," was all she'd say. Apparently Colton had stopped putting frogs down her neck or wrestling with her in the dirt. When Geoff saw the Chisholm boy in town with a girl named Jessica Granger, he knew that was the real heartbreaker for his daughter.

That's when he decided to get her out of Whitehorse. They both needed a change and that city life might be just what his wife would have prescribed for the problem.

But a part of him knew that she'd never gotten over her first taste of love—no matter how heartbreaking it had been. Is that another reason he'd wanted to come back here? He wanted his daughter to move on. He'd hoped her seeing Colton Chisholm again would do the trick.

As he studied Halley now, he saw a young woman who was equally at home in the city and the wild country of Montana. He hoped Mary Lou would be proud—he certainly was. But she still hadn't gotten Colton Chisholm out of her system. He was beginning to fear that she never would.

"Are you handling the case?" he ventured to ask.

"With the help of the state crime investigators out of Missoula. Don't give me that look. I believe a man is innocent until proven guilty."

"Even Colton Chisholm?" he asked, raising an eyebrow.

She gave him that crooked smile of hers, the one he suspected had gotten to the young, overly exuberant Colton Chisholm all those years ago. "Time will tell, won't it?"

He nodded, not worried. Halley was the

fairest-minded person he knew. But what if Colton Chisholm was guilty of murder?

Her cell phone rang and he saw her face as she checked the caller ID.

"It's the crime team. I have to take this." She took a breath before she said into the phone, "Deputy Robinson."

He watched his daughter nod, then turn away. "What did the coroner say? A teenage girl? Cause of death? Uh-huh. Any identification on her? Right. I'm sure we should be able to get DNA from her family. Thank you for letting me know. "

"They found that girl's body," he said as Halley snapped her phone shut.

There was a look of determination on her face, the same one he'd seen when she'd announced she was going into law enforcement.

"They found a teenage girl's remains in a grave not ten yards from where her purse had been buried," Halley said. "Seems Colton Chisholm was right. Jessica never left their secret spot that night. The question is— Who did?"

WHEN COLTON GOT THE CALL the next morning, he was on a narrow dirt road, driving down to check some fence he'd thought might be down because several cattle had gotten out.

He'd been trying to keep busy, but it was impossible not to think about Jessica and wait for the call he knew was coming.

Checking the phone, he saw it was from the deputy and no doubt the one he'd been dreading. He slowed the pickup to a stop, his heart pounding, and flipped open the phone. "You found her."

"You don't sound surprised. Why is that?"

He started to hang up. He was in no shape right now to argue with Halley about his guilt or innocence or anything else. While he'd been expecting this call, it had still hit him hard.

"Don't leave town."

"I told you, I'm not going anywhere." He snapped the phone shut, feeling the effect of the news like a second blow. The moment he'd found Jessica's purse, he'd known she hadn't left that spot that night without it. He'd known then that something bad had to have happened to her.

But what? It made no sense that someone would kill her—let alone kill her there. No one else knew about their secret spot. Unless someone had followed her that night. Someone like her father.

Fury forced aside the heart-wrenching pain. Someone had murdered Jessica and his baby. He couldn't depend on Deputy Robinson to catch the killer—not when she appeared set on nailing him for the crime. He knew she'd called in the state crime investigators, but this was a cold case—fourteen years cold. What was the chance that they would be able to find the killer?

He was going to have to find the culprit himself.

Colton got the pickup going again, his mind racing. Who knew Jessica was going to their secret place that night? Earlier one of the Grangers had mentioned that Jessica had called her friend who had a car the day she disappeared.

Twyla Reynolds. She'd been Jessica's friend since the first grade, the two as different as night and day. As he recalled, Twyla had married some guy who worked on the gas rigs up by the Canadian border.

It took Colton several seconds to remember the man's last name. Brandon. Troy Brandon. He drove into town and stopped by the sheriff's department first to pick up the copy Halley had made him of Jessica's letter and to borrow a phone book. Back in the pickup, he tried the number. Twyla's line rang four times. He was about to hang up when she answered.

"Hello." He could hear little kids yelling in the background. *"Hello?"*

Colton hung up and headed for the address he'd found in the phone book.

EMMA HAD ALWAYS appreciated irony. It hadn't escaped her that while she'd been busy plotting to help her stepsons find the perfect mates, her own love life might be on the skids. Earlier she'd wanted to confront Hoyt and demand to know what that conversation had been about.

But she hadn't. She told herself she couldn't bear the truth—not after just making love with Hoyt in the hayloft.

This morning, she felt foolish for not clearing up the matter right away. She trusted her husband. Of course nothing was going on. Still, she couldn't shake the nagging feeling at the back of her mind and the memory of the way her husband had turned his back on her all those times to take a call.

She thought of the strange phone calls she'd gotten. The parties on the other end of the line had been local women. Was it possible he was getting some calls like those, too? She should tell him about the calls she'd gotten. So what was stopping her?

She'd held her tongue because she knew it would hurt him deeply to hear that the community would say such things to his new wife.

But Emma had to bring all of this to light and ease her mind. She hated that she felt a little wobbly, not as if someone had knocked the legs out from under her, as she had last night. But still not herself.

Something was going on with her husband, that much was clear, and it had something to do with a woman. She hadn't heard him come to bed last night, so it must have been very late, and he was gone early this morning after leaving a note that said he would be mending a fence up north and wouldn't be returning until supper time.

DEPUTY HALLEY ROBINSON HEARD the despair in Colton's voice when she'd called with the news. Did she really believe that he'd killed that girl? Or was it that she didn't want to believe it?

The law enforcement officer in her was determined to do everything she normally would in a case like this. Halley reminded herself that this wasn't her case, but that wasn't going to stop her. She had to know the truth.

One thing that was bothering her was that lost letter from Jessica. It seemed like too much of a coincidence for it to turn up now—after fourteen long years.

Colton hadn't had to come forward with the

purse or the letter for that matter. Those actions did appear to be those of an innocent man.

But if he was guilty of the murder, then maybe it had been eating him up all these years and when he'd gotten the letter, he'd broken.

Except the part that seemed broken was his heart. He had looked devastated yesterday.

But what nagged at her about the letter won that it proved nothing. He still could have met Jessica fourteen years ago. He still could have killed her.

Halley swung by the Whitehorse Post Office. Whitehorse was one of those small Western towns that had sprung up next to the tracks when the railroad had come through more than a hundred years ago. The first Whitehorse, now known as Old Town Whitehorse, was about five miles to the south, near the Missouri River Breaks.

The newer Whitehorse was only about ten blocks square with more churches than bars, a small weekly newspaper, a hardware store, several gas stations and a grocery store. The town sat on Highway 2, what was known as the Hi-Line.

As Halley pulled into the post office parking lot, she noticed that there were always more pickups parked around Whitehorse than cars. Ranching and farming kept the town alive, but only barely. She wondered again at her father's determination to come back here—and, more to the point, why she'd decided to return here, as well. She told herself that she didn't like the idea of living hundreds of miles from her father.

She refused to admit that it had anything to do with Colton Chisholm, a possible murderer.

The postmistress was busy in the back sorting mail. Halley rang the bell on the counter and waited. A few seconds later, Nell Harper came out.

Halley explained that she was interested in a recent lost letter and asked about the things that had been bothering her. How was it that the envelope had a postmark on it, but he hadn't gotten it all those years ago?

The elderly postmistress shook her gray head. She seemed as perplexed as Halley.

"Where exactly was it found?"

"One of the patrons said she saw a corner of it sticking out from between the wall and the counter. When I saw the postmark, I couldn't believe it."

"How could the letter have been there for the past fourteen years?"

Nell shrugged. "I guess it somehow fell down between the counter and the wall and just now worked its way out. It's a mystery to all of us, that's for sure."

"I assume something like this doesn't happen often?"

"Good heavens, no. Mail gets lost occasionally, but finding a letter after that much time…"

Yes, that's what bothered Halley. First the letter, then the purse, then Jessica's remains. It just seemed too coincidental. It was almost as if the killer had choreographed the whole thing so they would find the girl. But was the plan to also cast suspicion onto someone else?

"Who found the letter? You said it was one of the customers."

Nell nodded. "To tell you the truth, I'm not sure who spotted it. Hazel Rimes pulled it out and handed to me. You might want to talk to her."

As she left the post office, Halley made the call but got an answering machine. She left her number, asking Hazel to call at her earliest convenience.

TWYLA REYNOLDS BRANDON answered the door in a pair of cutoff jeans and a food stained T-shirt and Colton realized he'd caught Jessica's former best friend either in the middle of breakfast or just finishing. It was hard to tell. Most of her dyed blond hair had escaped from the scrunchie-held ponytail. She had a dish towel in one hand and a baby bottle in the other. And there was quite a large amount of drying food on her T-shirt. He couldn't even guess what kind.

"Colton Chisholm?" She said it as if he was the last person she ever expected to find standing on her doorstep.

That alone pretty much summed up their relationship in high school. He'd never liked Twyla and most of it was because of the stories Jessica told him about her. According to Jessica, the girl had been wild and promiscuous and confided all of it in detail to Jessica, who in turn had shared the stories with him.

"You shouldn't be hanging around a girl like that," he'd told Jessica.

She'd gotten her back up and quickly defended her friend. "Twyla's had a hard life. You have no idea what her home life is like. Anyway, I don't see what is wrong with her just wanting to have some fun—you know, cut loose and enjoy life. I like her."

He'd let it drop but he'd never understood why they had stayed friends. It had bothered him more than he'd let on. He'd convinced himself that Twyla was probably lying about her exploits with boys and even some older men. The fact that she would never give Jessica names proved it. That and the fact that as far as Colton knew, Twyla had never even had a date in high school.

Now he realized it wasn't even the lies Twyla came up with that had bothered him. It was the fact that Jessica seemed to enjoy telling him all about her friend's alleged sexual exploits, even when he'd told her he didn't want to hear about it.

"I need to talk to you," Colton said now, all too aware that Twyla had known that he hadn't liked her. Was it possible Jessica had told her that he'd tried to get her to end the friendship? Now he feared that Jessica had confided in Twyla as freely as her friend had in her.

At the sound of something breaking deep in the house, Twyla looked behind her. Colton could hear swearing, yelling and crying. Along with the noise came the strong scent of burned oatmeal, which could explain some of the stains on Twyla's T-shirt.

She turned back to him, stepping out of the house and closing the front door behind her. "Why would you want to talk to *me?*"

He wished there was somewhere they could talk besides the porch. The windows were open to the house and he could hear what must be her husband arguing with the kids.

"It's about Jessica," he said.

"Jessica?"

He thought by now the entire county would have heard about the remains found north of town and was thankful that Twyla apparently hadn't.

He held out the letter. "Go ahead. Read it."

She looked at the page as if she wished he hadn't forced it on her. After a few moments, she took it and read it.

Colton watched her face, wondering how much she had known fourteen years ago.

Partway down the page, her gaze shot up to him, then returned to the letter.

What had surprised her? "You didn't know she was running away?" Maybe he'd been wrong about Jessica confiding in her friend.

She hesitated. "I guess it doesn't matter now. Sure, I knew she was running away but...not with *you*."

Colton stared at her, thinking he must have heard her wrong. He let out a humorless chuckle. "Who else would she have run away with?"

Twyla shrugged. "One of the others."

"Others?"

The woman looked at him as if he was the stupidest man alive. "You really didn't know? Seriously? When Jessica told me that she told you everything—and pretended *I* was the one who did…all those things with those guys—I thought for sure you were just playing dumb. But you really never caught on?" She shook her head. "So all this time you thought it was me." She gave him a pitying look. "You really didn't know your girlfriend, did you?"

Yesterday he might have argued that. But not today.

EMMA STARED DOWN AT THE top drawer of her bureau.

"Is something wrong?" Hoyt asked as he came into the room, startling her. His note had said he wouldn't be home until supper time.

She'd been putting away clothes fresh from the dryer and now realized that for several minutes she'd been standing there frozen to the spot. "Have you been in my drawers?"

Her husband chuckled as he came up behind her and put his arms around her. "Not yet, but I do like the sound of that."

"I'm serious, Hoyt. Someone has made a mess of everything in here." Emma liked things nice and neat, and just yesterday these drawers had been that. Now they had been rummaged through, as if whoever had gotten in them had been looking for something.

He let go of her and came around to look in

the drawer where she had been staring. "Who would go through your things?"

She glanced over at him, hearing something in his voice. Fear? One look at him and she could see that he was upset. "What's going on?" she asked.

He cleared his throat. "Nothing, it's just that in my haste, I spoiled the surprise. I was looking for your favorite nightgown to check out the label so I could see if the shop had anything else in that brand."

Emma felt terrible. "Oh, Hoyt." She hugged him, resting her cheek against his broad chest. When she pulled back, she saw something in his eyes that made her feel even worse. He looked angry. "I'm sorry I spoiled your surprise."

"No, I'm the one who's sorry." He closed the drawer and pulled her to him. "I should have been more careful."

He kissed her slowly. It had always been like this, from their first kiss, from the first time he had touched her she'd been lost.

"Hoyt, the laundry is never going to get put away at this rate," she pretended to protest as he pulled her over to the bed.

"In a few moments, laundry better be the last thing on your mind, Mrs. Chisholm."

And it was.

It wasn't until later, after Hoyt had gotten a call and had some ranch business to tend to, that Emma had found herself standing alone again at another one of her open drawers. Why would Hoyt have gone through all her bureau drawers if he had merely been looking for her nightgown? He would have found it in the second drawer with the rest of her pajamas.

Emma thought of that moment of anger she'd seen in his eyes just before he'd kissed her. She couldn't shake the feeling that someone else had been in her house—and her husband, even though he was angry with that person, was covering for him or her.

With trembling fingers, she looked in her jewelry box. Nothing was missing, but again, someone had moved her favorite earrings from where she kept them. Same in the closet where the hangers were all shoved back, as if someone had been looking for something on the floor or the shelves behind the clothes.

Hoyt? That seemed unlikely, even with his story about surprising her.

That's when she caught a whiff of an unfamiliar perfume. It dissipated almost at once, but she knew that she wouldn't forget the scent if she ever smelled it again.

Someone had been in the room. Had searched it even though that made no sense.

What could someone have possibly been looking for?

For a moment, she studied the room. Nothing was missing, as far as she could tell. But for whatever reason, her husband had lied to her about it. She'd seen how upset he'd been when he'd looked into the jumbled drawer and it hadn't been because she'd spoiled his surprise. No, this was like the secret calls he had to take, the conversations he didn't want her hearing.

And why had he come home early this morning after saying he wouldn't be back until supper time? He hadn't said and she hadn't gotten a chance to ask, she thought as she stepped to the window to see him take off in his pickup.

Where was he going in such a hurry? Emma feared it was to see the woman who used the unfamiliar perfume. She hated to think what kind of hold the woman might have on her husband.

Chapter Five

"Why should I believe you?" Colton said, taking a step back, as if he could distance himself from all this.

Twyla shook her head. "You've always thought I was a liar. Why change your opinion now?" She grinned. "Jessica told me she loved telling you what she'd done, all the details. She used to laugh at how shocked you were. It was all the more fun for her because you didn't know she was talking about herself."

Colton leaned against the porch railing for support. Inside the house, the swearing, crying and arguing had reached a new level.

"I've got to go..." Twyla didn't move, though. He could tell she wasn't in a hurry to go back in. She was enjoying herself at his expense.

He thought of the stories Jessica had told him about Twyla's conquests. And all the time it had been Jessica? He thought he might be sick.

"Who was the father of her baby?" he asked, his mouth dry as dust, his voice sounding strange to his ears.

Twyla merely shrugged. "She said it was some guy who picked her up one night when she hitchhiked into town. He was just passing through. That's why she needed to hit the rest of you up for money. She wasn't planning on keeping the baby. She was splittin' town alone, she told me."

He thought of the single bus ticket in her purse. Why had Jessica written him that she wanted to run away with him? According to Twyla, to hit him up for money. Clearly, she planned to leave alone. He could see himself letting her go alone that night, sending her money until they could meet up. He realized now that she wouldn't have been waiting for him in some town up the road, though.

Twyla seemed to realize that the copy of Jessica's letter still in her fingers and handed it back. "She told me you were her last resort. If she couldn't get what she needed from the others…"

"I get the picture." He thought about the first time he and Jessica had made love, her tears and his guilt that he'd taken her virginity. "I wasn't the first, was I?"

Twyla shook her head. "Her first, she told

me, was when she was fourteen. Some older guy who'd been helping out at the ranch that summer."

Fourteen? He closed his eyes for a moment, squeezing them shut.

"She must have told you who the others were," he said.

Twyla shook her head. "That was the one thing she never told me."

"Then there is a chance she could have been lying about all of it," he said, knowing he was clutching at straws.

"You should let it go. What's the point after all this time?"

"Even if she wouldn't tell you, there must have been someone you suspected," he pushed.

She studied him. "You want proof." She seemed disappointed in him, then angry. "Why don't you ask your buddy Lance?"

"Lance Ames?" He choked out the words. "Now I know you're lying."

Twyla smiled as she opened the door to go back inside.

"Lance wouldn't—"

"Jessica went after whatever she wanted, including Lance," she said, opening the door. She paused in the doorway. "Since Lance was your best friend, she thought it would be a kick. Even if he'd told you, you wouldn't have believed him. If it makes you feel better, she had to get him drunk and he couldn't stand the sight of her afterward, but she didn't care. She got what she wanted."

How could Twyla be talking about the sweet, innocent girl he'd thought he had to protect? "If any of this was true, someone would have told me. It's nearly impossible to keep secrets in a small town."

She laughed at that. "You mean the way Lance told *you?*"

He suddenly had a vague recollection of a time in high school when he and Lance had gotten into some argument. They hardly spoke for months. With a start he realized when that had been—when he'd been wrapped up in Jessica. They had gone back to being friends soon after she'd allegedly left town.

"Jessica liked older men because they weren't about to talk," Twyla was saying. She gave him another pitying look. "She told me that you thought *I* was a bad influence on *her.* We used to laugh our butts off about that."

Twyla was still laughing as she stepped back inside the house and slammed the door behind her.

EMMA DID HER BEST thinking at a small café on the edge of town called the Whitehorse

Café. This morning she took her usual table at a booth in the corner so she could see the door and have a view of everything that was going on.

In small towns like Whitehorse, the local café was the place to catch up on all the latest goings-on. Today though, because of the hour, the café was nearly empty. Only a couple of men were at the counter having coffee and talking about the cost of feed versus what you can get for a cow on the hoof.

Emma tuned them out. She had other things on her mind. Between worrying about her husband and her stepson Colton—

The café door swung open on a gust of cool morning air and Emma looked up to see a young female deputy enter. Since, as far as she knew, Whitehorse County had only one female deputy, this must be Deputy Halley Robinson, the woman determined to send her stepson to prison—if not the electric chair. If Montana had an electric chair.

"Excuse me, deputy," Emma said as the young woman started toward the far end of the counter.

The deputy turned toward her table and Emma got a good look at Halley Robinson. Her first thought was that she was much too pretty to be in law enforcement, let alone anyone who would want to hurt Colton. That sexist thought surprised her.

"Please, won't you join me?" Emma said and motioned to the booth seat across the table from her. "I'm Emma and I hate sitting alone."

She saw the young woman hesitate.

"Late lunch or just coffee?" Emma motioned to the waitress who came right over.

Deputy Robinson reluctantly slid into the booth. "Just coffee."

"Please have something to eat. April, bring us a couple of plates and a piece of that home-made apple pie." Emma quickly turned to the deputy. "Unless you'd rather split the banana cream?"

Halley Robinson smiled. "April, why don't you bring me the banana cream and Mrs. Chisholm the apple pie."

"So you know who I am," Emma said, liking the humor she saw in the deputy's big brown eyes. She could see why Colton had been so enamored of this woman when she was a girl. She must have been adorable because she was a beauty now. And smart, too. "But please call me Emma. I have a feeling you and I are going to be great friends."

COLTON FOUND LANCE AMES in the corral at the Flying Double A Ranch. Lance had inherited the ranch from his father and now raised some cattle, but his real love was horses.

"Hey, Colt, you're just in time," he said as he led a filly around the corral. "Have you ever seen a more beautiful horse?"

"Come out of the corral."

Lance stopped, his smile quickly disappearing. "What's wrong?"

"Out of the corral."

Lance called to one of his hired hands to take the filly back to her stall before he climbed the corral railing to jump down next to his friend. "It isn't your old man, is it? I heard he got remarried?"

"Dad's fine." Colton looked into the face of his best friend and told himself Twyla had lied. "I need to ask you something."

Lance shoved back his hat. "Fire away."

"Were you ever with Jessica?"

Colton saw the change in his friend's expression. He let out a curse an instant before he drew back his fist. The blow caught Lance in the jaw and sent him staggering back.

"Hold on," Lance said, raising both hands in surrender.

"You were my friend."

"I'm your *best* friend," he said. "If you recall, I tried to warn you about her."

"Warn me?" Colton took a step toward him. Hell, yes, he remembered now. That's what they'd had the argument about. Lance had tried to bad-mouth Jessica, and Colton wasn't having any of it. He'd thought his friend was just jealous. "You did a hell of a lot more than just try to warn me, didn't you?"

Colton took a swing, but Lance dodged it and caught him with a fist to the temple that made him see stars.

"I don't want to fight you, but I damn sure will," his friend said. "She wasn't the girl you thought she was."

He swore. "I keep hearing that and maybe you weren't the friend I thought you were."

Lance shook his head. "I guess that's a two-way street if you're going to believe Jessica over me."

Colton felt all the pain and anger and frustration surge inside him. He charged, barreling into Lance and taking them both to the ground. They fought as they had as boys, until Lance caught him in the ribs and, seeing the pain in his friend's eyes, rolled away from him.

"You okay?" Lance asked as Colton managed to lift himself up into a sitting position.

He thought about his stepmother telling him he was too old to be rolling around in the dirt. She was right.

After a moment he caught his breath and the pain in his ribs ebbed a little. "Jessica's dead." He saw Lance's shocked expression. "Someone killed her fourteen years ago. She was pregnant, but according to her friend Twyla, it wasn't mine."

Lance shook his head, his gaze taking on a faraway look. "It wasn't my baby if that's what you're thinking. I don't know what you heard, but Jessica put something in my drink at that party at the bridge you missed the fall of our junior year. The party that got raided by the sheriff."

"I remember how drunk you were, and upset. I thought it was because your old man had to bail you out of jail and grounded you."

Lance shook his head. "I swear I didn't even know what was happening until after it was over."

"You should have told me."

"Yeah," his friend said. "I tried and you might remember how that went. I figured Jessica would tell you. You should have seen the triumphant look on her face. I knew she'd only done it to come between you and me. And it worked."

Colton didn't think he could feel any worse. He was wrong. Lance had been his friend since grade school and he trusted him with his life. "I'm sorry."

"Me, too," Lance said as he rose and offered Colton a hand up off the ground. "This all must have come as a real shock."

"Yeah." Colton took his friend's hand and let him pull him to his feet. He bent to pick up his hat from the ground. He told Lance about the letter and his visit to Twyla. "It isn't bad enough to find out that someone apparently murdered her that night. Now I find out that Jessica wasn't the girl I thought she was. I actually thought I was protecting her."

Lance shook his head. "Jessica was one messed-up girl."

"Yeah, I'm starting to realize that, and I think it all goes back to her family, her father in particular."

"Are you sure she was even pregnant?" Lance asked.

"I don't know. Her family believes it." He thought about some of the things Twyla had told him. "Apparently she liked older men." He remembered that Jessica had told him about an older, married man Twyla was seeing and had hinted that it was someone they all knew.

"Someone killed her and, if she was pregnant, then I suspect it was because of the baby," Colton said as he dusted himself off. His ribs hurt like hell and he was afraid he'd chipped a tooth. He really had to stop this. "I'm going to find the bastard."

"Shouldn't you let the sheriff do that?"

"The sheriff's not in town and the case is being handled by the state crime team. Deputy Halley Robinson is involved up to her pretty little ears and I'm her number one suspect."

Lance let out a surprised sound. "Not that girl—"

"Yep."

"You really do have a hell of a time with women, don't you?"

HALLEY HAD TO HAND IT to Emma Chisholm. She didn't mention Colton or the murder case the entire time it had taken them to have their pie and coffee.

Instead, the attractive older woman had steered the conversation to everything from a good piecrust recipe to the surplus of wildflowers this year to what it takes to be a deputy.

Emma had listened as if truly interested in Halley's training. "Did you always want to be in law enforcement?"

She'd explained how she'd taken some criminal behavior classes in college and gotten hooked. Before that she hadn't had a clue.

Then Emma had gracefully steered the

conversation back to pies. "I hope we get some good apples this year. Do you have apple trees?"

"My father does in his yard. He bought a small ranch south of town," Halley said, surprised that she was enjoying the woman's company. "I rent an old farmhouse just outside of town. I haven't even looked to see what's growing in the yard."

"Well, if you have crab apples, let me know. I've been wanting to make a batch of crab apple jelly. I'd be happy to share."

They'd parted company out by Halley's patrol car. It wasn't until she was driving away that she realized how much Emma Chisholm had gotten out of her about her personal life.

The woman was so darn likable and self-deprecating that Halley had opened up, something she usually didn't do.

Now, though, she wondered what Colton Chisholm's stepmother had really wanted. Halley realized that she should have been more circumspect. The problem was that none of the questions Emma had asked had felt as if she was prying. She seemed genuinely interested.

Halley shook her head. All morning she'd been thinking about Colton because it had become obvious quite quickly that he was looking into her investigation. The man just didn't take no for an answer. And neither did his stepmother.

She found herself following his trail, first to Twyla Reynolds Brandon, Jessica's former best friend, and then to Lance Ames.

Twyla told her a story about Jessica's exploits, one that Halley couldn't help but react to with skepticism. The girl was a liar. She'd certainly lied to Colton. Why wouldn't she lie about everything else?

"This wild sex life that your friend had— are you sure she didn't make the whole thing up?"

"Maybe. Or maybe that's what got her killed. The last time I saw her she told me she was going to try to get money out of all of them. She said they couldn't very well turn her down, not when she told them she was pregnant."

Halley studied the woman sitting in a ragged recliner, a baby in her arms and several other small, dirty children hanging off the side of the chair. The house was a total disaster and Twyla looked as if she was fifty instead of thirty.

Twyla had been envious of her friend—that much was obvious. Was that why Halley was having trouble believing any of this story?

"Anyway, why would she lie?"

"To make herself more interesting?"

Twyla shook her head. "I think she used sex to control men. Or maybe it was all about defying her parents. Can you imagine what her father would have done if he'd found out?"

Halley could after spending just a short amount of time with Sid Granger. "I assume you told Colton about this when he stopped by?" Clearly, Twyla would have relished every word.

"He used to treat me like dirt."

"Wasn't that because Jessica told him you were the one sleeping around and he believed her?"

"I suppose," she said grudgingly.

"So your friend really didn't do right by you, telling such stories about you. Didn't some of the boys at school think they were true and try—"

"That wasn't Jessica's fault," Twyla snapped. "It was Colton's. He's the one who talked about me to the other boys."

Halley didn't believe that. "However it happened, it all goes back to Jessica and the lies she told about you."

Twyla said nothing, just looked scornfully down at the baby in her lap.

"It wasn't that big a deal," she said finally. "Jessica and I used to laugh about how we were fooling everyone, especially Colton."

"I'll bet you did." Halley couldn't help but think about how mean kids could be at that age.

It had been a relief to leave Twyla's house and the sour smell of baby spit-up and bitterness to drive out to the Ames ranch. The land stretched out as far as the eye could see. Halley put down her window, letting the warm summer air rush in.

Unfortunately, it did nothing to alleviate the bad feeling that had been growing with each person she talked to about Jessica Granger.

She found Lance Ames out by the corral. He had a cut over his left eye and a bruise along his jaw.

"I see Colton has already been here," she said, followed by a silent curse. She remembered Lance from school. He'd always been nice to her although he was Colton's best friend even then. She wondered if they were still best friends. The cut over the eye said otherwise.

"I need to know what you told him," she said, taking out her notebook and pen.

"You should talk to *him,*" Lance said. "It was personal."

"I can see that. Why'd he hit you?"

"If you think this is bad, you should see him." The joke fell flat.

"You slept with Jessica."

Lance shook his head. "I told you—"

"Do you think he killed Jessica?"

"No way."

Halley nodded. "So he didn't know before now that you slept with Jessica."

Lance groaned. "She seduced me at a party. Truthfully, I'm surprised that anything happened, as drunk as I was."

That explained the cut and bruise. "So you're telling me—"

"I don't believe I was telling you anything."

"Why are you covering for him?"

"I'm not. You're wrong about Colt. He's the best man I know. He didn't do anything to Jessica but try to help her. It's Jessica you need to be looking into. That girl was seriously messed up."

Halley saw the guilty look Lance tried to hide. "You knew what Jessica was like but you didn't tell Colton."

He sighed. "I tried. It almost ended our friendship."

"He loved her that much?"

"It wasn't love. Jessica used him. She made him think he was the only one who could save her."

"Save her from what?"

Lance shook his head.

"Come on, help me out. If you really believe Colton is innocent, then help me. Who was she sleeping with besides Colton?"

He looked off toward the Larb foothills for a moment. "I saw her come on to a guy, a mechanic in town who was old enough to be her father." He made a disgusted sound.

"She came between you and Colton. You must have hated her."

Lance laughed. "I stayed as far away from her as possible."

"Did she hit you up for money?"

"Even Jessica wasn't that stupid."

"Why are you worried about your friend if you're so sure Colton is innocent?"

"Because I know him. He's determined to find out who killed Jessica."

"Why would he do that now that he knows she lied and cheated on him?"

"Colt feels as if he failed her."

Halley took that in. "How's that?"

"She was having some kind of trouble at home. Colton thinks her behavior was a cry for help and that he should have done something to save her."

"He told you this?"

Lance laughed. "Yeah, right. Colton has

always been so forthcoming." He shook his head. "He didn't have to tell me. He's my best friend. I've known him since kindergarten."

"You didn't tell him about the mechanic." Lance shook his head and she could see that he was worried what his friend might have done with the information. "What's the man's name?"

"Deke Hanson."

"Is he still around after fourteen years?"

"Never left. He works at the garage in town."

EMMA FOUND HOYT SITTING on the porch when she returned home. She climbed the steps to take a seat next to him on one of the half dozen old oak chairs and rockers that had been in his family apparently for centuries.

The first thing she noticed was how quiet it was and asked, "Where are your sons?"

"Got them all out workin' except for Colton. Don't know where he is."

Something in his tone made her look over at him sharply. She'd promised herself that she wasn't going to ask. Better not to know. But that wasn't her way. "What's going on, Hoyt?"

He looked out across the land as if he never got tired of staring at it. The country up here was lush and green this time of year. In the distance, huge cottonwoods formed a green canopy over the Milk River, both winding their way toward the Missouri. Emma had fallen in love with the area the moment she'd seen it. Just as she'd fallen for Hoyt Chisholm.

"I know something other than the obvious is bothering you," she said and braced herself for the worst. "You might as well spit it out."

He smiled then and her heart broke at the sadness she saw in his blue eyes. "I did somethin'." She wanted to take her question back. She couldn't bear what Hoyt was going to say. "Fourteen years ago Jessica Granger contacted me. She told me she was pregnant with Colton's baby, but that she would give it up for adoption if she had the money to start over."

"Oh, Hoyt." Emma felt such a wave of relief, tears welled in her eyes.

"I knew better than to pay her off," he was saying. "But I couldn't let this girl ruin my son's life and you know damn well she would have."

Emma nodded. On that they could agree.

"Ten thousand dollars."

She let out a low whistle. "In *cash?*"

"Of course in cash. When we never saw her

again, I thought she'd done just what she'd said she was going to do. I can't tell you how many times I've thought about that baby…" His voice broke.

Emma stared at her husband, seeing how hard it had been for him to go behind his son's back, but even harder to give up his own grandchild that way. Hoyt loved kids. That's how he'd ended up with six adopted sons, and it was no secret that he couldn't wait until this ranch rang out with the sounds of little cowboy boots.

After the initial shock and relief that this was at least part of the reason Hoyt had been acting so strangely, Emma felt the weight of what her husband was telling her. Her mind began to whirl with the possible consequences of his actions.

"Does anyone else know?" she asked, wondering if the calls he'd been getting involved blackmail.

"No."

Emma knew she should have been relieved. "Colton said there was only $200 in her purse when he found it."

Hoyt nodded. "Maybe her killer took the money."

Emma felt her heart lurch at his words. "Hoyt, tell me you didn't meet that girl the night she died."

Chapter Six

After her visit with Twyla Brandon and Lance Ames, Halley was getting damn tired of finding herself trailing behind Colton. He was interfering with her investigation and it was time she set him straight on a few things.

She'd tried to call Hazel Rimes again, the woman who had allegedly found the letter from Jessica to Colton between the wall and counter at the post office. Still no answer. She left another message.

Halley couldn't shake the feeling that the letter played some important part in all this. She was suspicious as to why it had turned up now after fourteen years. It just seemed too coincidental somehow. The same with Colton finding the purse.

The problem was that she couldn't understand why, if he had killed Jessica, he had come forward with it. At first she'd thought that he was racked with guilt. Guilt did strange things to people. But she'd seen his expression when he'd found out that Jessica had been pregnant. His shock, his devastation, his anger had all been real.

She couldn't even imagine what he was going through now—given what Twyla Brandon had told him about Jessica and his fistfight with his best friend, Lance Ames. By now he must know that, according to Twyla, he wasn't the father of the baby, but then Jessica could have lied about that as well.

Halley worried that Colton Chisholm was a loose cannon, jumping on his big white horse and riding off to avenge Jessica's murder—no matter what she'd done to him. According to Lance, Colton blamed himself for not saving the girl.

But what exactly had Jessica needed saving from besides herself?

Whatever Colton was going through, Halley couldn't have him playing hero. The fool didn't seem to realize that he was chasing someone who'd already killed once and had gotten away it. There was more than a good chance that the person would kill again to keep that secret.

When she spotted his pickup coming out of a side road, she turned on her siren and lights and went after him. She caught his angry expression in his rearview mirror as she pulled him over to the side of the road. Climbing out of the SUV, she walked up to the driver's side of his pickup. He whirred down his window and gave her a disdainful look.

"There is no way I was speeding, so what the hell are you—"

"Your license, registration and proof of insurance, please, Mr. Chisholm."

"You aren't serious."

"Sir…"

He groaned as he dug out his wallet and then rummaged around in the pickup's glove compartment before handing her the documents she'd asked for. She studied each for a long moment, giving him time to settle down before she handed them back.

"Mr. Chisholm—"

"Aren't we past that?" he interrupted. "We've known each other since grade school."

"You're interfering with my investigation, Mr. Chisholm, and if you continue—"

"What are you going to do? Arrest me? Hell, you've been wanting to do that ever since you got back into town. So let's get it over with, *Deputy Robinson*." He shoved open his door, forcing her back, as he got out.

She started to reach for her weapon, but he merely held out his wrists. "Put the cuffs on. Take me in. Charge me." His voice dropped to a dangerous seductive level. "Or help me find Jessica's killer."

She started to open her mouth to tell him that it was her job to find the killer, not his, but he cut her off before she could get the words out.

"The only way you're going to be able to stop me is to arrest me," he said, that warm brown gaze locking with hers. "So let's do it."

"I'M NOT GOING TO ARREST YOU."

"Oh, yeah?" Colton said, worked up now. He knew he was on dangerous ground, but he couldn't help himself. He'd been through too much in the last twenty-four hours. "You'd better arrest me," he said advancing on her.

"Easy, Colton," she said, raising a hand as she stumbled back until he had her trapped against the side of the patrol SUV. "You don't want to do anything you'll regret."

He laughed. "Is there really anything I could do that would make you any more convinced that I'm a killer?" When she didn't answer instantly, he said, "That's what I thought."

"You're wrong."

He laughed. "Nice try. But too little too late and not very damn convincing." He pulled off his hat and raked his hand through his hair in frustration. "I know what this is really about. It's about me making a complete fool of myself back in grade school, isn't it?"

"This has nothing to do with a few frogs down the neck."

"Like hell," he said, stuffing his hat back on his blond head before he pressed his hands on the warm metal of the SUV on each side of her, trapping her against her patrol car. He knew he was about to step over a line that he couldn't uncross, but he didn't care.

He was so close to her that he could see into the depths of her dark brown eyes. "You have that same look you did in grade school when you were about to slug me. Hell, now though you can just shoot me."

"Colton," she said in warning but there was a hitch in her throat as his gaze shifted from her eyes to her full bow-shaped lips. Every lick of common sense in him begged him to stop, but he was too worked up and damn but this woman had always had this effect on him.

He dropped his mouth to hers. He felt her gasp and then he was tasting her, pressing her against the side of the patrol SUV, intensely aware of the soft curves of her body. He felt her respond to the kiss, swore he could hear the pounding of her heart in sync with his own.

But as he drew back, he expected to find that old fire in her eyes that was pure anger.

Colton braced himself for a blow. Or worse the cold, hard steel of her gun barrel pressed against his already sore ribs.

But what burned in her eyes wasn't anger.

He heard a vehicle coming up the road and stepped back. Halley moved away, her back to him as a ranch truck passed, kicking up a cloud of dust.

"I'm sorry," he said to her slim back after the dust had settled. He was still shaken by the kiss, but all his earlier anger was gone. Now all he felt was an aching desire to kiss her again.

"I'll bet you're sorry," she said, turning to him again. Her face was flushed and he wondered if she was half as rattled by that kiss as he was.

"I'm not sorry about *kissing* you," he said. "I'm sorry about the way I treated you when we were kids. But you were just so impossible."

"Impossible?"

"Yes, impossible. I liked you, but every time I got near you, all you wanted to do was slug me or wrestle me to the ground."

Halley was shaking her head. "Apparently, you don't recall that you were the one who started it with your frogs and your—"

"I was a kid," he snapped. "And then we weren't quite kids anymore and I didn't know how to change things between us from what they'd been and you sure didn't make it easy. I liked you. But, quite frankly, you were as intimidating as hell."

"But Jessica Granger *wasn't*."

"No. She… I really don't want to talk about her with you."

Halley shifted on her feet, looked off for a moment, then settled her gaze on him again. "You have to stop looking for her killer."

He shook his head. "So we're back to that?"

"Colton—"

"I know. Stay out of your way."

"No, that isn't what I was going to say." She seemed to hesitate. "Instead of running ahead of me, how about helping me?"

He stared at her. "Is this some kind of trick?"

"No trick. Maybe I'm just tired of fighting you."

He couldn't help but grin. "That I will never believe."

"Well, believe this. I don't want to see you get arrested or, worse, killed."

He felt a ridiculous jolt of pleasure at her words. "So you're worried about me?"

"Surely you realize that whoever killed Jessica thinks he got away with it. If you continue digging—"

Colton laughed as he stared at the deputy. "You just admitted that you don't think I killed her."

TWENTY MINUTES LATER, Halley was still mentally kicking herself as she stepped from the hot sun beating down on the pavement to the cool shade of the automotive garage. Her face still felt blistering hot, but not from the summer heat. Her run-in with Colton had knocked her for a loop. And that damn kiss…

She touched her tongue to her lips, then caught herself and swore under her breath. If only she could quit thinking about all the things he'd said. She'd *intimidated* Colton Chisholm? He'd *liked* her? She knew it was silly. Hey, it had been junior high, but it still gave her a small thrill at the thought, which she quickly quelled. She was acting like the tween she'd been, and while it made her heart beat a little faster, she still had a killer on the loose that she was now more desperate than ever to find.

All her instincts told her that Colton hadn't done it. She felt a chill, though, as she remembered how her instincts had failed her not that long ago. There'd been another suspect she'd trusted back on the West Coast. She shivered at the memory of how close she'd come to getting killed because she'd fallen under the spell of the suspect. Her throat tightened at the memory.

One kiss and suddenly she believes Colton is innocent? Apparently, she hadn't learned anything from that earlier brush with death.

The garage smelled of grease and clanked with the sound of metal tools. There were three vehicles, one up on a hoist, the others with their hoods up, but no sign of anyone.

"Deke Hanson?" she called into the cavernous space. She had to yell again over the sudden loud whirl of a high-powered drill as one of the mechanics loosened a bolt.

A head appeared as a man rolled partway out from under one of the vehicles in the second bay. His face was smudged with grease, his dark eyes small in a web of squint lines. She estimated his age at somewhere in his late forties. "Yeah?"

Halley watched his gaze focus on her as she approached. First the uniform, then her face, then her chest. She saw his expression turn from worry to amusement. Some men seemed to think there was no reason to be concerned about a woman deputy. Apparently Deke Hanson was one of them.

"Deke Hanson?" she asked.

"In the flesh."

"I'm Deputy Robinson. I'd like a word with you." She realized that all the noise had ceased and that the other two mechanics were waiting to see what was going on. "In private."

Deke sighed and shoved off the side of the car to propel himself all the way out from under it. He got awkwardly to his feet, something she could see bothered him.

"I'm a little stiff today," he said, leering at her. One of the other mechanics chuckled from under a neighboring vehicle. "Big baseball game yesterday. I'm the star hitter." Another chuckle.

"Why don't we speak in your office?" Halley said and waited for him to lead the way.

"So what's this about?" he demanded once she'd closed the office door. Without his buddies around to hear him, he'd dropped the cuteness.

"Jessica Granger." She saw his eyes narrow, his jaw tense.

He licked his lips. "Who?"

"Your girlfriend fourteen years ago."

Deke looked away as he let out a bark of a

laugh. "Honey, I've had a lot of girlfriends in the last fourteen years."

"It's *Deputy* and I think if you give it a moment you'll be able to recall Jessica. High school junior. Big age difference. Statutory rape."

"I never touched her."

"Oh, so you do remember her."

He swore under his breath. "Believe me, you don't forget a girl like that. She's the one who came on to me. Girls like that you have to fight off with a stick."

"Apparently, you didn't have a big enough stick."

He raked a greasy hand through his already greasy hair. Halley wondered what Jessica had seen in this man fourteen years ago. He would have been old enough to be her father back then.

"I already told you," he said defiantly. "I never touched her. She was a kid. I'm not stupid."

That was debatable.

"So you're saying you didn't get her pregnant?"

"Pregnant?" He laughed and she saw him relax a little. "That definitely wasn't me. After my wife popped out three in less than four years, I fixed that little problem. It's been

sixteen years. You don't believe me, check with my doctor."

She did believe him. "But vasectomies don't always work so that doesn't exactly clear you, does it?"

He shook his head as if she just didn't get it. "The girl came into the garage with her *father"*

"You aren't telling me that she flirted with you in front of him."

"That's exactly what I'm telling you. I think she was just trying to get a rise out of him."

"And did she?" Halley asked, disturbed by the picture she was getting.

"She sure as hell did. He couldn't get her out of here fast enough. He threatened to whip my ass if I ever came near her. The bitch lost me a client. He never came back in again."

"And you never saw her again?"

"You better believe it. That girl was trouble and her old man... He was one scary dude when he lost his temper."

Her cell phone rang. She took it outside, letting Deke Hanson get back to work. Her warrant for Jessica Granger's medical records had come through. Finally, she would know whether or not Jessica had really been pregnant.

COLTON WASN'T SURE HOW he should feel about Halley admitting that she didn't think he was a killer. Relief, sure, but he was still insulted that she had even considered that he might have murdered Jessica in the first place.

He was also a bit taken aback that she'd said she needed his help. That, he thought, was probably just to get him to quit looking for the killer on his own.

Whatever her reason, it hadn't dissuaded him in the least. He owed Jessica this and the more he'd thought about Jessica and who might have killed her, the more it brought him back to why she was running away in the first place. Something was going on at that house, specifically with her and her father.

It wasn't unusual for a father to be protective of his daughter, but Sid Granger seemed to have taken it over the top. Was it possible his overprotectiveness, if that's all it had been, had pushed Jessica to do the things she had?

Colton was convinced that Millie Granger knew the truth about what was going on in that house and why Jessica was so desperate to get out of it.

He called, ready to hang up if Sid answered. To his relief, Millie picked up on the second ring. "It's me, Colton Chisholm. I need to talk to you about Jessica."

"Yes." From the odd way she said it, he could only assume that her husband was nearby.

"Can you get away to meet me?" he asked, figuring that she might talk without Sid standing over her. "Say twenty minutes at…" Where? It had to be a place they could talk where it wouldn't appear they had planned the meeting if it got back to Sid. "The grocery store." He could hear her ready to say no. "Or I can come to your house—"

"No, that's quite all right."

Twenty-five minutes later she joined him at the back of the grocery store. She pushed a metal food cart and kept looking around as if she was afraid she'd been followed.

"You shouldn't have called," she whispered, after making sure no one was close by. This time of the afternoon, the small store was practically empty.

"You lived in that house with your daughter," Colton said. "You had to know what was going on with her."

As someone crossed the aisle at the other end, Millie took a box of crackers off the shelf and dropped it into her basket. "What are you saying?"

"I wasn't the only one your daughter had been with, was I?"

She looked away.

"You *knew* your daughter was promiscuous?"

"I can't talk to you about this." She started to step away, but he stopped her.

"You have to talk to me. You accused me of knocking up your daughter and then killing her because I didn't want to marry her. Was she even pregnant?"

"Yes. That isn't something she would lie about."

"Oh, really?" he snapped, keeping his voice down. "She lied about everything else. Who was she seeing besides me?"

She shook her head.

"Jessica told me about some older, married man," Colton said. "She swore it was Twyla who used to sneak out of the house and meet him at night when his wife was sleeping. He had more to lose than anyone if he thought he'd gotten an underage girl pregnant."

Millie tried to step past him, looking stricken. "Please, I can't bear to hear this."

"Why are you protecting this man? Your daughter is dead. I would think you'd want to expose him."

"Sid and I did the best we could." She started to turn away.

Colton grabbed her thin arm and was surprised at the strength he felt there. "You *both* knew?" He felt her tense and let go. "Oh, my God."

She suddenly looked panicked. "It isn't what you think. Her father loved her. Everything he did, he did it because...he had to." She spun around, banging her cart into a stack of cookies. Several packages toppled off to the floor, but Millie Granger didn't slow down as she rushed off, one of the wheels on her grocery cart squeaking loudly.

HALLEY HAD JUST ASSUMED that Dr. Brian "Buck" Carrey was one of a long line of doctors who'd come to Whitehorse on his way somewhere else. The doctors were usually young, stayed only a short while, then moved on to greener pastures.

But when she stepped into Dr. Carrey's small office, she was surprised. The older man behind the desk looked as if he'd be more at home on the range than behind a general practitioner's desk. He wore a cowboy hat over his long gray ponytail. His face was tanned and weathered with deep lines around his eyes.

He broke into a huge smile as he pushed back his hat and considered her. "When they told me I had a deputy waiting for me… I had no idea it was going to be a filly."

Halley wondered if she would ever get used to this. Most places didn't think twice about a woman being in law enforcement. But then Whitehorse, Montana, wasn't most places. She could well imagine what the townsfolk thought about having a woman as sheriff.

"Dr. Carrey, I have a warrant to see the files of Jessica Granger," she said, getting right to business. "The last time she was in would have probably been about fourteen years ago."

"Before my time and call me Buck," he said before turning to call, "Margaret?" An elderly nurse appeared in the doorway. "Going to need some old files." He swung his gaze back to Halley. "Jessica Granger, that right?"

She nodded.

"I'll have to go over to the storage space," Margaret said. She was plump, in her sixties with short gray hair and a pleasant face.

"I'll go with you," Halley said handing her the warrant.

The files were stacked by date in a large storage unit that smelled of dust and age. It didn't take Margaret long to find Jessica's file.

"Did you know Jessica Granger?" Halley asked.

"I remember her," she said as she handed over the file. "I was sorry to hear that she might have been murdered."

But not surprised. Just as Halley wasn't surprised that word of the murder was out. News traveled at the speed of wildfire in a windstorm through Whitehorse.

"So you *knew* Jessica?" she prodded.

"I wouldn't say that," the nurse said quickly. "I knew *of* her." She clamped her lips shut as though she wished she hadn't said that.

Halley opened the file, thumbed to the back, past the usual childhood injuries and illnesses, to Jessica's last doctor visit. She glanced from the page up at the nurse in surprise. "She *wasn't* pregnant." Relief flooded her. It was bad enough that the girl had died, but at least there hadn't been a baby involved.

This would be a relief to Colton as well. She couldn't help the thought. She'd seen how hard he'd taken the news that not only his girlfriend, but possibly also his baby, had been murdered. Even though Twyla had sworn it wasn't his, Halley was sure that Colton would always wonder.

Something caught her eye. "What's this about a call to Social Services?"

"Counseling, I would imagine."

"What for?"

The nurse hesitated before she said, "Possible physical abuse."

"She had bruises on her arms and strap marks as if she'd been restrained and *whipped?*" Halley said, reading the doctor's notation on the chart.

"She told the doctor—"

"Yes, I see what she told the doctor," Halley said as she turned the page and saw the notation. "She said it was a sex game she played with her boyfriend and he got a little rough? Is there any truth to this?"

Margaret shrugged. "She had a tendency to…"

"Lie?" No kidding.

"Prefer fiction over reality, possibly. When she came in, she was convinced she was pregnant and very upset that she wasn't."

Halley felt sick. Something had been terribly wrong with this girl. "Did you believe her, that the injuries were from a sex game?"

Margaret again hesitated before she met her gaze. "I can only tell you that the doctor decided a call should be made to Social Services and that the family should be…interviewed."

So the doctor thought something was wrong at home, as well. Flipping back through the file, she found a note indicating that the doctor had called Jessica's father. The note said the father had been defensive. "Was Social Services ever called? I can't find any notation that they were."

"You'd have to check with them."

Back at the doctor's office as Halley waited for a copy to be made of Jessica's file, she thought about her visit to the Granger house yesterday. The vibes at the house had been more than a little tense. She thought about Millie nervously kneading at her faded apron and the hole in it where the fabric had torn. There was something definitely off in that house.

But she reminded herself that Jessica's parents had just found out that their daughter was probably dead. She couldn't imagine what that would do to the family dynamics, especially since Jessica had been their only child.

Then again, something had been wrong long before that, since Jessica had been running away.

At the Social Services Department, Halley was led by the receptionist into a small, hot room at the back. The woman behind the desk introduced herself as Alice Brown. When Halley showed her the copy of Jessica Granger's referral sheet, she said she was familiar with the case.

So the doctor *had* called. "I need to know

what you found out when you went to the Granger home."

"I never went. I was informed by the mother that Jessica had run away. I filed a report and that was the last of it."

"You never investigated it further?"

"Jessica was out of the house," she said defensively. "Whatever was going on there, without her testimony, there was nothing I could do," Alice said.

"What do you suspect was going on there?"

The woman shook her head. "If Jessica returns…"

"That isn't likely, since someone killed her the night she tried to run away."

All the color drained from the social worker's face. "Oh, no. You don't think the father…" She shuddered at the thought.

So did Halley.

AS COLTON LEFT THE supermarket after his brief rendezvous with Jessica's mother, his head was spinning. He'd seen the panic in Millie Granger's eyes. She was clearly terrified of her husband and Colton was sure now that Jessica had been leaving to get away from her father.

He climbed into his pickup and sat for a moment, trying to decide what to do next.

"What the hell had been going on in that house?" he said to himself as he recalled the bruises he'd seen on Jessica before they'd gotten into the argument that last night he saw her.

"Who did that to you?" he'd demanded. Jessica had insisted that they meet at their secret place after dark. He wouldn't even have seen her injuries if she hadn't flinched when he touched her. He'd turned on the flashlight he'd brought to make his way back to his pickup later and had been shocked.

It wasn't the first time he'd seen bruises on her, but she always had an explanation. This time there was no explaining away the marks.

"I asked you who did this to you?" he repeated.

She moved away from him, covering the welts on her legs as well as the bruises on her arms. "Leave me alone."

"I can't. I want to help you," he said, kneeling down next to her.

But she'd pushed him away. "I told you to leave me alone. You tell anyone about this and I'll swear that you did this to me."

For a moment, he'd been too shocked to speak. "You wouldn't do that."

"Oh, yeah? Try me and you'll be sorry you ever met me," she'd snapped.

"I'm already sorry." He had grabbed his jacket and the blanket and left.

Now he felt desolate. Why hadn't he told anyone? He might have saved her life.

His head whirling, he started out of town toward home. He was thinking about swinging by the Grangers' on the way and confronting Jessica's father when his cell phone rang. It was Halley Robinson.

"What now?" he snapped.

"Is that the way you always answer your phone?" she asked.

"Only when I see that it's you calling," he said, then regretted it. "Sorry, I'm just not up for more bad news."

"I don't think what I have to tell you is bad, but either way, I still need to talk to you," she said.

He sighed. "I need to talk to you, too. I just had an interesting conversation with Millie Granger." He heard the deputy make a disapproving sound. "Look, you need to hear about this." He knew he had to tell her about the bruises, but he was hesitant. Jessica had threatened to make him look guilty—and now he had no way to prove otherwise. Colton knew that Sid Granger would deny laying a hand on his daughter. At this point, even Sid might be more believable to the deputy.

"Where are you?" Halley asked. "I'd prefer not to discuss this on the phone."

"I'm on the way to the ranch…" He squinted at the cloud of dust he spotted ahead. Out of the dust came a pickup. His father's. He saw Hoyt slow ahead and wave through the open window for him to stop. He had a bad feeling that his father had been coming to find him. Something was up.

"Is there somewhere we can meet?" Halley asked. "Is everything all right?" she added when he didn't answer, distracted by his concern about what his father might want.

"Just great," he said as he watched his father get out of his pickup. Colton slowed, seeing something in his father's face that set his heart racing. "I can't talk right now."

"Jessica wasn't pregnant. I thought you'd want to know."

He stopped on the edge of the road. His father was waiting for him, standing in the middle of the narrow dirt road, looking as if the weight of the world was on his shoulders.

Jessica wasn't pregnant. Maybe all of it had been a lie. Maybe…

"I didn't mean to blurt it out," Halley

said. "I just wanted you to know. I thought it would—"

"I really can't talk right now." He snapped the phone shut and got out of his pickup.

As he stepped to the middle of the dirt road, his father looked up and Colton saw his expression. His blood turned to ice.

Chapter Seven

"Son," Hoyt said as Colton joined his father in the middle of the road.

"What's wrong?" Clearly this was about something that couldn't wait.

Hoyt pulled off his Stetson and raked a hand through his graying hair. When his father had first returned to the ranch with his new bride, there had been a lightness to his step. Emma seemed to have taken years off him. But right now, in the harsh sunlight, Hoyt looked all of his fifty-six years and then some.

"I need to tell you something."

"And you thought in the middle of the road would be a good place?"

His father sighed as he pulled his hat back onto his head. "There is no easy way to say this. Jessica called me fourteen years ago."

"Why would Jessica call *you?*"

Colton listened, his pulse rising with each word as his father told him. He'd seen the fear

in Hoyt's eyes and had known this was bad—
he'd just never expected this.

"You paid her off?" He swore, turning
away from his father, afraid what he would
do. He couldn't believe this. "What if Jessica
was pregnant with my child?' He swung back
around, fisting his hands as he scowled at his
father.

"You were *seventeen*," Hoyt said.

"I don't give a damn. You had no right."

"Go ahead, take a swing," his father said
as Colton stepped forward. "Get it out of your
system. Can't say I wouldn't feel the same way
if my old man had done what I did."

Colton wanted to. But a man didn't hit his
father. He stood, shaking with rage. He'd been
angry with Hoyt Chisholm before, many times,
but never as angry as he was now and it scared
him. He'd lived long enough to know that what
either of them might say or do right now could
destroy their relationship. He loved his adoptive father and that love kept him from saying
the angry things inside him.

Hoyt had adopted him and his fraternal twin
brothers, Logan and Zane, after their mother
had died in childbirth. He'd raised them and
three other sons mostly by himself all these
years. Colton could never forget how different his life would have been if it wasn't for

the generosity and love that Hoyt had shown him. He often forgot that they didn't share the same blood because this man was their father and always had been.

"I met her the night she disappeared and gave her the money, just as she asked," Hoyt said.

Colton was shaking his head. "Don't tell me you met her at—"

"The spot where I understand her remains were found. I had no idea the two of you had been meeting back there. Don't look at me like that. I didn't touch a hair on her head." His father's obvious disgust for Jessica felt like another blow.

Everyone had seen through Jessica but him, the dumb kid in love. The dumb kid who thought he would protect her because, as young as he'd been, he'd instinctively known that Jessica needed protecting.

"I wanted to tell you before I told the deputy," Hoyt said.

"You're only going to make yourself a suspect." He knew his father couldn't have killed Jessica, but that didn't mean Halley would believe it. "Deputy Robinson already has it in for me. Now she can add my family."

"You don't have to tell me how stupid I was—especially given what happened to

Jessica that night. I'm sorry, I didn't like her, can't pretend I did. I probably shouldn't have given her the money, but I knew you, Colton. You would have married her even if it wasn't your baby."

"She wasn't pregnant. She lied."

His father nodded, not looking surprised in the least. "Even if she had been pregnant, she didn't have any business raising a baby. I thought I was doing what was best for my grandchild—*and* my son."

"Don't ever make that mistake again," Colton said and stalked back to his pickup. Once behind the wheel, he saw his father walk slowly back to his own pickup, his head down.

Colton swore and slammed his fist down on the steering wheel. Then he started the engine and left in a cloud of gravel and dust.

HALLEY THOUGHT AT FIRST it was Colton calling her back. She knew she shouldn't have been surprised that he was still digging into Jessica's death, but he had to be careful talking to Millie Granger. If her husband found out—

Where had that thought come from? From her growing suspicions about Sid Granger.

Checking her phone, Halley saw that it was the sheriff's department dispatcher calling. She said she had a call from Hoyt Chisholm and patched it through. She was surprised that he hadn't called sooner. The rancher had a lot of clout in the state. She wondered if he would try to strong-arm her into searching for suspects other than his son. Or if he would try to charm her. She'd heard he did both well.

Deciding it was time to find out, she said, "I'm out your way. Why don't I stop by?"

"Actually, it might be easier if I came to you, since I'm not at the ranch house. I'm on my way into town."

She spotted his truck coming down the road toward her and looked for a place to pull over. She wasn't sure that meeting him in the middle of nowhere was the best idea, but it was too late to do anything else as she saw him slow down.

Pulling over into a wide spot beside the road, Halley braced herself for the confrontation she knew was coming. As Hoyt Chisholm pulled in, she got out of her patrol SUV. This face-off would be bad enough with him standing beside her SUV or even worse if he got into her patrol car. She preferred standing, although he would tower over her five-foot-five frame.

He cut the pickup engine and got out, walking toward her slowly. He looked like a beaten man. So this was the way he planned to play it?

"There's something I need to tell you," he said after introducing himself and shaking her hand. His grip had been strong and he'd met her gaze with a steely blue one.

"If this is about Colton and my investigation—"

"It's about Jessica. I met her that night and gave her $10,000, at her request, to leave my son alone."

Halley had *not* been expecting this. For a moment she was at a loss for words. "Where did you—"

"At the spot where I heard you found her remains."

She was taken aback by this information, especially by how freely it was given.

"She was alive when I left her there. I had the feeling that she was waiting for someone else," he said, then seemed to straighten to his full height as if a weight had been lifted off his shoulders.

"The money wasn't found on her."

Hoyt nodded. "Colton told me there was only $200 in her purse. I have no idea what happened to the money I gave her."

"You didn't change your mind when you saw

her? Get angry? Decide there was another way to keep her from ruining your son's life?"

He smiled then and Halley thought that while Colton might not be Hoyt Chisholm's son by birth, he'd definitely acquired his adoptive father's charm. "Would I have come forward if I'd taken my $10,000 back that night?"

Once she was over her initial shock, she said, "You had more motive to want her dead than your son did. Is that why you're coming forward now, to try to shift suspicion away from him?"

"Isn't it possible I just had to tell the truth? I thought that girl had taken the money and left town." Hoyt rubbed a big hand over the back of his neck. "No matter how I felt about her, my son cared about her. I want to see her killer caught because of that."

He sounded so darn sincere, she actually found herself believing him. "What time of night was it when you left her there?"

"About eleven-thirty."

"What was the money in?"

"A large paper bag. The bills were hundreds. Old ones I took out of my safe."

"You're in the habit of keeping $10,000 in old hundred-dollar bills in your safe?"

He smiled again. "I do like to have some cash on hand. That particular money, though, was from the sale of a bull. I'd been paid with the old hundreds and I just hadn't taken them to the bank."

Halley remembered years ago hearing about one of the Chisholm bulls that had gone for $30,000. Cattle were Hoyt Chisholm's business and he'd done well by it.

"I appreciate your coming to me with this information," she said. "I may need to ask you further questions in the future."

"You know where I live."

EMMA HAD MADE A QUICK trip into town after Hoyt left, telling herself that she had to make tonight's dinner extra special.

When she returned home, she hadn't been surprised to see that all the ranch pickups were gone and Celeste hadn't arrived yet to help with supper. Hoyt, she knew, had gone off to find Colton. The rest of his sons were working somewhere on the ranch.

She had no idea where any of them were— including her husband. The thought had never crossed her mind before that she should worry about where they were. She'd always known that they would all show up come supper time. If they were moving cows, sometimes they didn't make it back for lunch, but they never missed supper.

Emma had brought fresh-cut flowers and the other necessities for the special supper she had planned. Celeste would pick up anything else they needed.

But as she stepped into the house, she stopped cold. At first she wasn't sure what had made her freeze just inside the door. Emma had never felt afraid alone out here on the ranch in the two weeks she'd been here. Even though it was miles from the next ranch and even farther from town, she'd loved the peace and quiet, the solitude.

She thought that was what was wrong with the world these days. People couldn't find solitude in the big city. That wonderful complete lack of noise and other people. It was why so many people always had a cell phone to their ear—they couldn't even stand being alone with their thoughts.

Now as she stood just inside the door, she could hear birds singing, the sigh of the breeze in the tall cottonwoods next to the house, a hawk crying out in the distance—and the pounding of her heart.

It took a moment to realize what had spooked her. Then she caught another whiff of it. Perfume. It was the same scent she'd caught just a hint of after someone had searched her bedroom.

Emma felt her heart drop like a stone. Another woman had been in her house again and she had a terrible feeling that Hoyt Chisholm knew exactly who that woman was.

COLTON HAD THOUGHT ABOUT skipping supper to avoid seeing his father. He was still furious with him, but he knew he'd have to contend with Emma if he missed the meal.

A part of him also realized after he'd calmed down some that he was going to have to face his father—and Emma. He had no doubt that Hoyt had confessed first to Emma. If she'd been around fourteen years ago, Colton was sure Emma would never have let Hoyt do what he'd done.

The moment he saw her, Colton knew that she'd been worried about the confrontation between father and son. She looked relieved to see him.

"We have company coming for supper tonight," she announced as she nervously straightened the bouquet of flowers at each end of the long dining room table.

Since Emma had come into their lives, there were flowers in the house and they dressed for dinner. Nothing elaborate, like tuxes, just clean boots, jeans and Western shirts. Hair combed.

Hats off. Everyone freshly showered. She even had Hoyt saying a prayer before they ate.

In just two short weeks, Emma had made some major changes at the Chisholm ranch. Colton had to hand it to her. She seemed to be good for their father.

He studied her now, though, with some concern. She was acting as if everything was fine, but he could see by the way she fussed over the flowers that she was nervous. Since he hadn't seen his father since their meeting in the middle of the road, he figured Hoyt had gone to Deputy Robinson to confess and that's what had his stepmother on edge.

With a silent curse, he realized that he hadn't called Halley back. He told himself he would after dinner. Right now he was too upset. In fact, his stepmother's words had only now registered.

"What company?" he asked, noting that there was only one extra plate set at the table. Was it just him? Or did this seem like a bad time to have dinner guests? But of course he didn't tell Emma that.

Emma hurried off to the kitchen as if she hadn't heard his question. Often they had cattle buyers join them for dinner. Emma always said, "The more the merrier." She was so different from other nonranch-raised women who hated living on a ranch so far from town, and especially hated all the cooking that went with ranches and their crews and visitors. A woman like Jessica.

Who, he told himself, was the last person he wanted to think about right now.

His father had just come in through the side door when the doorbell rang. Emma came flying out of the kitchen, her expression one of anticipation and nervousness. The nervous part wasn't like her and Colton found himself looking toward the living room where his father had gone to answer the door.

He heard the door open, then nothing but what seemed like an awfully long silence.

"Please come in," Emma said, rushing to the guest at the front door. "Supper is almost ready. We're delighted you could join us."

"Emma?" Colton heard his father say and, unable to stand it any longer, got up to see what was going on.

His brothers had just come in through the back and looked expectantly toward the front of the house as if they knew something he didn't.

Colton spotted a car he didn't recognize parked out front an instant before he saw Deputy Halley Robinson standing in the doorway. *She* was their dinner guest?

Halley wore a pale yellow sundress that accented her dark hair, brown eyes and tanned skin. Her long hair, normally pulled back and tied up when she was on duty, now hung around her bare shoulders in soft curls.

He stood staring in wonder at how amazing she looked and realized his brothers were doing the same thing. A sharp pang of jealousy jolted him. Where had that come from? Halley Robinson sure as hell wasn't his.

Emma proceeded to go around the room introducing each of her stepsons.

As she came to Colton, he said, "We've met," and wondered what the hell the deputy was doing here. Clearly, someone had invited her to supper.

"Halley and I ran into each other in town today," Emma said, apparently realizing an explanation was needed. "I invited her to join us for supper."

"That was thoughtful of you," Hoyt said, an edge to his voice. He, no doubt, was wondering what the hell his wife had been thinking inviting the deputy sheriff who wanted to see either his son or himself fry for murder. Or both.

"Why don't we all have a seat?" Emma said.

The entire evening Colton felt as if Halley

was watching him. He couldn't shake the feeling that she'd come out here merely to confirm her worst suspicions about him and his father.

He hated most that the whole time he'd been too aware of her every movement. For all his focused attention on her, it could have been just the two of them in the room. He'd barely touched his food and felt awkward and self-conscious, as if on a first date.

Nor had he said more than a few words and only those because Emma had been determined to include him in the conversation. He'd been afraid to open his mouth for fear of what might come out. He kept thinking about kissing Halley.

At Emma's suggestion, after supper was finally over, he walked Halley to her car. Not that he hadn't already planned to see the deputy out. "What was *that* about?"

She looked surprised. "Supper?"

"You know damn well what I mean."

"Your mother and I ran into each other today in town. She invited me and I took her up on it."

"She's my stepmother and I don't want you around my family."

Halley raised a brow. "It was just supper."

"You came out here to investigate."

She laughed. "Oh, you mean that story your *stepmother* told about you jumping off the roof onto a horse like you'd seen on television when you were five? I'm just trying to figure out how to use that against you." Halley shook her head and a sadness came into her gaze. "I had a good time. Please thank your…Emma for me again."

They both turned at the sound of the screen door banging open. Emma came rushing out with a foil-wrapped package and handed it to Halley.

"I thought you'd like the last piece of apple pie."

"No, I couldn't—"

"Take it to your father. You're doing me a favor. I can't have my stepsons fighting over it," she said with a wink.

"I was just asking Colton to please thank you again for inviting me," Halley said. "I really enjoyed it and the meal was amazing."

Emma glowed in the praise. "You must come again soon." With that she turned and hurried off.

"I'm sorry you think I had an ulterior motive for coming out here tonight," Halley said. "Your stepmother is very persuasive. If anyone had an ulterior motive though, it's Emma."

"What are you talking about?"

She shook her head as she opened the door to her car, climbed in and drove off.

Colton had to move back or she would have run over the toes of his boots. He watched her drive away, her last words echoing in his head, and realized he hadn't told her about his talk with Millie Granger.

EMMA SAW COLTON'S EXPRESSION as he came back into the house and couldn't hide her disappointment that the evening hadn't gone as well as she'd hoped.

She'd thought that once the deputy saw Colton with his family, she would realize there was no way this young man could be a killer. She'd invited Halley to supper before Hoyt had dropped his bombshell. But she hoped that the deputy also realized after a nice meal at the ranch, that neither Colton nor Hoyt had anything to do with that girl's death.

"I'm glad Halley had a nice time," she said, just because she needed to say something as Colton came toward her.

She thought for a moment that he might tie into her but instead, he glanced past her, snapped his mouth closed in an angry line and, turning on his heel, headed out the front door.

She sighed and turned to find her husband

standing behind her with a similar look on his face. No wonder Colton had taken off the way he had. "Emma, what were you thinking?"

In retrospect, she had no idea. Her new family had all acted oddly at supper, all of her stepsons but Colton flirting with Halley, and her trying to cover for both Hoyt's and Colton's silence.

"She seems like a nice young woman," was the best defense she could come up with.

Hoyt shook his head, pushed past her and took off toward the barn.

Emma sighed again, then turned back toward the kitchen, needing to work off her disappointment as well as her fear. Both Colton and Hoyt were furious with her. Both were suspects in a murder case and Emma worried that was only the tip of the iceberg.

She knew she was just trying hard not to think about her own worries since smelling the perfume in her house a second time.

As she began cleaning up the dishes, she thought maybe the night hadn't been a total disaster. She recalled the times she'd seen Halley Robinson steal a glance toward Colton.

It wasn't the look of a lawman at a suspect. Unless she'd lost her mind, Halley liked her stepson. Maybe more than the woman wanted to admit.

Emma just hoped she hadn't made things worse. But then how could it be any worse with both a son and his father now suspects and her fearing her husband was lying to her about... well, possibly about everything.

"HOW WAS YOUR EVENING?" Geoff Robinson asked his daughter when she stopped by his house to give him the piece of apple pie.

"Interesting," she said as she kicked off her sandals and tucked her legs under her on the couch, as she'd done since she was a little girl. She hugged herself as she watched him eat the pie.

"This is delicious. Please thank Mrs. Chisholm."

Halley nodded but seemed lost in thought, a small smile curling her lips.

He would have loved to know what that was about. "Anything new on the case?" He was instantly sorry he'd asked because the smile vanished.

"No. Just more disturbing information. Jessica wasn't pregnant. She apparently lied to get money from the men she was sleeping with—and Colton's father. Worse, it appears she was being physically abused. Possibly sexually abused."

"By someone in her family?"

His daughter frowned. "Probably, although Jessica tried to implicate her boyfriend. I can't rule out Colton Chisholm, even though I really like his stepmother and the rest of his family."

Wisely, he merely nodded. A day ago Colton would have been at the top of her list as a suspect. Clearly, something had happened to change her mind about him. Her father wondered what as he saw her touch her fingers to her lips and that small secretive smile appear again.

Her cell phone rang and she quickly checked it. "I have to take this." She got up and walked outside barefoot to the patio. A breeze stirred the new green leaves of the cottonwoods. In the distance, the Little Rockies had turned a deep, dark purple against the fading light. This far north it didn't get dark this time of year until almost ten.

Geoff Robinson finished the pie and waited for his daughter, praying that returning to Whitehorse had been the right thing to do—and, in turn, talking Halley into coming back here as well.

He'd thought it would be safer for her than out on the West Coast where she'd been working as a deputy—and had nearly been killed. But as he watched her, he knew she'd gotten more information about the Jessica Granger case and it wasn't good news.

"That was one of the investigators from the state crime lab," she said when she returned.

"Something wrong?"

"I need to go back to the crime scene. The state investigators are wrapping it up there. Not much evidence is left after fourteen years." She sighed. "A cold case like this…there's just little chance it will be solved and the suspects, well, they'll live the rest of their lives with everyone in town believing they're guilty."

He knew she meant Colton Chisholm. "Honey, you can only do so much. Maybe when the sheriff gets back—"

"I'm not going to stop digging into the case," she said, pocketing her phone and giving him a smile. "With Jessica's purse and her remains discovered, the killer has to be worried. With a little push, who knows what will happen?"

Geoff Robinson was suddenly hit with a terrible premonition that coming back to Whitehorse had been a mistake.

Chapter Eight

The crime scene was bathed in twilight when Halley passed under the yellow tape. The team was packing up to leave.

A van with more techs had driven up from Missoula to take back the remains and the crime team. The lead tech told her that they had scoured the area for evidence all day, but after fourteen years there didn't appear to be anything to find.

She thought about taking a look at the crime scene herself, but she was dog-tired. If there had been anything to find here at the scene, she knew the crime techs would have found it.

She thanked them and left. By the time she pulled into her driveway in front of the old farmhouse she'd rented on the edge of Whitehorse, all she could think about was going to bed. It had been a long day. Not to mention emotionally exhausting.

She smiled at the thought, since kissing Colton Chisholm shouldn't have been that exhausting. Nor should having supper with his family. But just being near him...

She shoved that thought away as she climbed out of her car. The house was too large for one person, but she was too old not to have her own place. She hated to think how she would be able to afford heating the big old rambling place come winter, but for now it felt like home. In truth, she'd liked it the first time she'd laid eyes on the house. It was just far enough out of town.

"It rents cheap," the realtor had told her.

Cheap was exactly what she needed.

"You'll want to look around for a place you can buy."

Halley didn't see that happening. When her father had moved back, bought a small ranch, and she'd seen an ad for an opening as deputy, it had seemed like a good idea. She knew he was worried about her after everything that had happened at her last job. She had to admit that she was still shaken by her near death at the hands of a killer—a killer she'd foolishly trusted.

But now she was involved in a murder investigation and one of the obvious suspects was the one person she wasn't sure she could be objective about.

Halley had so much on her mind that she didn't notice at first that someone had jimmied her front door.

With a curse, she stepped back onto the porch and walked as casually as she could to her patrol SUV. Popping the lock, she opened the door and reached inside for her shotgun. As she closed the door quietly, the shotgun in her hands, she glanced toward the old farmhouse, listening.

The only sound was the breeze in the lilac bushes. It rustled the leaves and sent the now sickeningly strong smell of lilac into the summer night breeze.

She retraced her steps, climbing the porch to the front door and then easing it open. There was no vehicle in the yard and her instincts told her that whoever had broken into her house was long gone, but she wasn't taking any chances.

Her first thought had been a burglar, but she'd quickly rejected that idea. Since arriving in Whitehorse, she'd had little time to do more than buy some used furniture. She didn't even own a television or sound system. The small radio in her kitchen wasn't worth stealing and she didn't own anything a decent burglar would consider good jewelry.

No, whoever had broken into her house wasn't there to rob her.

Halley moved through the house, her weapon drawn. Her mind raced. It made no sense that someone would break in, so she figured it must be kids and that meant vandalism.

But as she searched each room, she saw no sign that anyone had been here. Nothing seemed to be missing or messed up.

As she neared the bedroom door, she slowed. The door was closed. She was nearly positive she'd left it open. Stepping to it, she took hold of the knob with her left hand, her right hand gripping the gun, and eased the door open.

The closet door was open—as she remembered leaving it. She glanced at the old vanity pressed against the wall. Her jewelry box sat on top, also open.

She could see even from where she stood that no one had been in it. One look and they would have noticed that she had very little jewelry and nothing worth stealing.

Realizing that the room was empty, she put her shotgun down and stood for a moment trying to reassure herself. No one was in the house.

But someone had been. Why? What had they been looking for?

She stood in the room, tired and irritable and a little spooked. The house felt different now. As a deputy, she'd worked with victims of burglaries and break-ins. The victims always said they felt violated, but she'd never had to experience it herself before. Mostly, it made her angry as hell.

She leaned the shotgun against the wall by the door, too tired to go back downstairs, even though she realized that she hadn't locked the front door. Not that it would matter since whoever had jimmied it had broken the lock.

Exhaustion pulled at her, even though it was still early. She stepped to the bed, wanting to just fall in under the covers without even undressing. As she tugged down the comforter, she heard the sound. Unfortunately, it didn't register until she'd uncovered what someone had left her.

COLTON MENTALLY KICKED HIMSELF as he started down the road away from the main house toward his own place. He hated the way he'd left things with his father, with Emma, with Halley. He'd been a jackass at supper.

But when he got around Halley, he had a history of doing everything wrong.

Except for the kiss. That had felt right, dammit.

He slowed at the county road, considering which way to turn. To the left and home? Or to the right and Halley's house? He knew the old farmhouse she rented just out of town.

He doubted that apologizing would get him anywhere with her. But he wanted to see her. He hadn't gotten the opportunity to tell her about his meeting with Millie Granger and his conviction that Sid Granger had lost his temper and killed his daughter when he'd caught her running away. He'd believed she'd gotten herself pregnant and had been furious about it.

Colton sat for a moment longer at the crossroads, finally giving up when he couldn't shake the feeling that he needed to tell Halley as soon as possible. He turned right, swinging the pickup onto the county road, and heading for her house. He didn't care what kind of reception he got. It wasn't as if he was expecting her to welcome him with open arms.

As he drove, his window down, the cool summer night air blowing in, he noticed the first few stars pop out in the expanse of sky that spanned the horizon. On many nights like this, he'd seen the Northern Lights and always felt awed by the light show nature put on this far north.

As he turned down the road to her place, he was glad to see that Halley's patrol SUV and car were parked in front. He pulled in and sat for a moment, half hoping she'd heard his pickup and would come out on the porch. Probably armed with a shotgun though, he realized.

When she didn't, he debated leaving. Maybe this hadn't been such a good idea after all. A scented breeze blew in his driver's-side window. He could smell the lilacs in her front yard, still fragrant for a little longer before they would be gone for another year.

He remembered the way Halley's hair had hung around her shoulders, the soft look in her brown eyes and what she'd said just before she'd driven off.

Holy hell. Had she meant that Emma was trying to set them up?

He was reaching for the key to start the pickup and get out of there when he heard the scream. It came from inside the house.

In a heartbeat he was out of the pickup and running toward the house.

EMMA LOOKED OVER, SURPRISED to see that Hoyt had forgotten his cell phone on the nightstand, as it vibrated. He'd been keeping it with him, even when he went to shower, but tonight he'd left the house and forgotten.

It vibrated again and she reached over and picked it up. It wasn't until it vibrated a third time that she opened it.

"Hello?"

The laugh was soft and seductive sounding. "You must be Emma."

"And you must be…?"

"Aggie Wells." A beat of silence. "I take it Hoyt hasn't told you about me."

Emma felt her heart drop, but she tried to keep the pain from her voice. "What exactly should he have told me about you?"

That laugh again. "Why don't we meet and I'll tell you everything. Hoyt has that cattleman's assocatiation meeting tonight. Shall I come out to the ranch or—"

"Why don't I meet you somewhere?" Emma suspected the woman had already been out to the ranch several times. The perfume. The rummaged chest of drawers. The feeling that someone had been in the house.

"You pick the place," Emma said.

"I don't know Whitehorse that much better than you do, but I think some place out of town would be better. Do you know the bar out at the Sleeping Buffalo? Since it's a weeknight and early, we'll have the place to ourselves."

"I'll meet you there in an hour."

"I'll be waiting. I'll be the woman—"

"Don't worry. I'll recognize you." Emma snapped the phone shut and put it back on the nightstand. Then she headed for her closet to decide what to wear to meet the other woman in her husband's life.

COLTON HIT THE DOOR AT A RUN. As he burst in, he heard a second scream. It sounded as if it came from upstairs. He took the stairs three at a time. At the landing he ran launched himself at the open doorway.

Halley stood, back against the wall, eyes wide, her face white with terror.

For an instant he was too surprised to take in what was happening. He'd never seen Halley scared before, let alone terrified.

Then he saw the snake. The rattler was coiled just feet from her.

He moved with a speed that even surprised him, grabbing the comforter off of the bed and dropping it over the snake.

The ominous sound of the rattling snake still filled the room as he quickly bundled it up in the comforter and carried it down the stairs and outside where he shook out the snake. It slithered off into the darkness and he turned and hurried back upstairs.

Halley was just where he'd left her.

As he stepped toward her, he saw that her face was still bloodless, her brown eyes wide.

"Come on," he said taking her hand.

She seemed to stir, but she was still trembling. "Where are we going?"

"Downstairs."

"The snake?"

"Long gone. I'll come back up and make sure there are no others in the room, then I'm going to make you something to help you sleep."

"Sleep?" she asked as if he'd lost his mind.

"Sleep. You're exhausted."

She shook her head as if the last thing she was going to get tonight was sleep.

"Don't worry. I'm staying tonight."

Her eyebrow shot up and he saw some of the old don't-take-any-guff Halley Robinson in her expression.

"I'll sleep on your couch or on the floor next to your bed, whichever makes you feel safe. I'm not leaving you alone until we can get some decent locks on these doors."

Some of the color came back into her cheeks. "I'm a deputy sheriff and I can—"

"I know. You can take care of yourself." He could see that she was embarrassed. "There is no crime in being afraid of snakes. Especially rattlers. Truth is, nothing scares me more than coming across one."

She cocked her head, clearly not believing him.

"Honest to goodness," he said and then led her downstairs to the kitchen.

She sat in one of the kitchen chairs while he checked the fridge, found milk and then a pan and began to heat the milk on the stove.

"Warm milk?" she asked, sounding amused.

"My dad used to give it to me when I couldn't sleep."

HALLEY HEARD THE CATCH in his voice and realized that his father must have confessed to him about trying to pay off Jessica. She could imagine how Colton had taken that news. She remembered how close he was with his father. She'd seen Hoyt pick up the boys from school. What kind of man adopted six sons to give them a good home? Apparently, a very kind, loving, generous one.

She knew that Colton's mother had died giving birth to him and his two brothers. Like her, he'd never known his birth mother.

"Are you all right?" he asked, studying her with concern as he stirred the pan of milk heating on the burner. He'd caught her glancing around the kitchen floor as if she expected to see more snakes.

"I. Don't. Like. Snakes."

"I remember, but I had no idea you were that afraid of them. Halley, I'm so sorry. I was such a jerk as a kid."

He had the most beautiful eyes. Between his eyes and his grin, was it any wonder she'd fallen for Colton so many years ago?

"Can you ever forgive me for what I did to you when we were kids?" he asked.

She wasn't about to tell him that when he stopped tormenting her, that was when he'd broken her heart.

"Here, drink this," he said as he put a cup of warm milk in front of her. "I'll be right back."

She picked up the mug, cupping it in both hands. The heat felt good, reassuring, just as Colton's presence in her house did. She liked having him here. The house felt almost cozy. She began to relax as she heard him searching upstairs.

Careful, girl, she warned herself. But how was she to know that she was a sucker for a man who came riding in to save the woman in distress?

She just never thought she would be that woman.

THE BAR WAS DARK AND empty just as Aggie had said it would be, except for the forty-something female bartender who was busy cutting up limes—and the woman sitting at a table in the back.

Emma had expected Aggie Wells to be young, blond and brassy. As she walked toward her, she had to work to hide her surprise and confusion. The brunette appeared to be about Emma's age, somewhere in her early fifties, and definitely not blond or brassy.

"So you're Emma," Aggie said, studying her, a slight smile on her face. "You're nothing like I expected."

The bartender called to Emma, asking what she'd like.

"Give her a stiff drink, honey," Aggie called to her. "She's going to need it." Aggie turned her attention back to Emma. "The usual? A margarita, blended with salt."

"You are certainly well informed," Emma said.

"Bartenders know everything," Aggie said with a grin. "The one at the hotel in Denver where you and Hoyt met is especially talkative—if you know what to ask."

"I'm touched that you have taken such an interest in my life," Emma said, trying hard to hide her surprise and her irritation. But she had to admit, she was just as curious about Aggie Wells.

Aggie wore a white long-sleeved shirt, open at the neck, and blue jeans. Her long legs were stretched out on the booth seat, her back to the wall, confidence in every line of her slim body, intelligence shining in her pale blue eyes.

Emma had the strangest thought. She would have liked this woman had they met in some other circumstance.

Aggie gave the order to the bartender, getting herself another bottle of beer with a tequila chaser. As Emma slid into the opposite side of the booth, Aggie drew her legs off the booth seat and turned to face Emma.

"Before you get me drunk, why don't you tell me what this is all about," Emma said.

"Fair enough. What do you know about your husband's past?"

Next to nothing, but she hated to admit it.

"Never mind. I already know he swept you off your feet, quickie marriage in Vegas." She made a disappointed face as if Emma should have been smarter. Emma was beginning to think the woman was right.

"Why don't you fill me in, since you seem to know a lot about my husband, as well as me. By the way, why is that exactly?"

"I'm the private investigator who's going

to prove your husband killed his last three wives."

Emma was too shocked to speak. She took a long swig of her margarita, licked the salt from her lips and told herself to breathe.

"I take it no one's mentioned the Chisholm Curse to you?"

Emma thought of the phone calls and lied. "No."

Aggie gave her an impatient look. "You don't know that Hoyt Chisholm's first wife, Laura, drowned in Fort Peck Reservoir and her body was never found?"

Emma knew his first wife had died soon after the two of them had adopted three little boys whose mother had passed away during childbirth. The father of the babies was unknown.

"I didn't know she drowned."

"On a fishing trip with Hoyt, just the two of them out in the middle of Fort Peck—a huge lake with more shoreline than California."

Aggie sounded angry.

"What is your interest in this?"

"I want to get the insurance company's money back," the woman said.

"Insurance?"

"Hoyt insured Laura and himself for a cool million."

Emma choked on her drink. Hoyt had said he needed to get an insurance policy on her. He'd said it was because she was now one of the owners of Chisholm Cattle Company. She'd agreed.

After a few moments Emma finally found her voice. "Of course the insurance company is going to want to believe it was more than an accident—"

Aggie smiled. "First wife, a million. Second wife, a million. Third wife, a million. See a pattern there?"

Emma didn't know what to say, since she hadn't even known about the other two wives. "Did your insurance company insure all three wives?" she asked.

Aggie shook her head. "Only the first one."

"Then how do you know—"

"I know. He didn't ask you to sign a prenuptial agreement, did he?" Aggie asked with a sly smile.

She knew her expression gave her away.

"That's the way he works it. No prenup, but he takes out insurance on them. If they try to leave him..."

"You don't know they tried to leave him."

Aggie gave her a pitying look. "Wife number one had filed for divorce before the boat trip. Wife number two had told several of her friends that she was leaving him. Wife number three—"

"Not every woman is cut out for living so far from civilization. Maybe I should have found out more about my husband before I married him," Emma admitted. "But I know that he loved me. That was enough."

Aggie raised a brow. "What if I told you his second wife, Tasha, died under suspicious circumstances and his third wife, Krystal, disappeared?"

"I'd say Hoyt has had some very bad luck with wives," she managed to say.

Aggie laughed. "Are you always this annoyingly cheerful?"

"Most of the time."

The P.I. shook her head.

"Look, Hoyt started to tell me about this past but I hadn't wanted—or needed   to hear about it. At this age, we all have a past we might want to forget."

"What if he killed his other wives and you're next?"

AGGIE COULD SEE THAT Hoyt Chisholm's new wife was having trouble breathing.

"I trust my husband." The words lacked conviction. "I know my husband."

Aggie laughed and drained her beer bottle and followed it with the shot of tequila and a slice of lime. She motioned to the bartender for another drink.

Emma declined. It was obvious that she was anxious to leave and get home and question her husband.

"That would be a mistake," Aggie said.

"I beg your pardon?"

"You can't wait to confront him." She shook her head. "Very bad idea. Don't you think the others did the same thing?"

"You told the second and third wives about your suspicions in the first wife's death?" Emma sounded shocked and outraged.

"They had a right to know who they were married to—and now they're dead."

"I thought you said his third wife was disappeared."

"Hoyt recently had her declared legally dead."

Aggie's drink arrived and she downed the tequila first this time, sucked for a moment on the lime before taking a long drink of her cold beer. It felt so good going down. Almost as good as it was going to feel nailing Hoyt Chisholm finally.

She realized that Emma was studying her intently. "Your insurance company doesn't mind your drinking on the job?"

Aggie merely smiled. "I like you. I'd hate to see something happen to you. Take my advice. Get as far away as you can from Hoyt Chisholm or you're going to end up as dead as the others."

"Have you actually *met* my husband?"

"I've seen him and we've talked a few times on the phone."

Emma smiled. "What are you doing for dinner tomorrow night?"

A few moments later, Aggie was still chuckling to herself as she watched Hoyt Chisholm's new wife leave the bar. Emma had more guts than the others, that was for sure.

She studied the woman's ramrod-straight back, the way she held her head high, the squared shoulders. A woman who couldn't be rattled.

If Aggie hadn't noticed the way Emma Chisholm held her purse, she might have bought the act.

Instead, she watched with strange fascination as wife number four hightailed it out of the bar. Emma Chisholm was running scared.

But not of her husband.

That was the part that fascinated Aggie.

With a jolt that made her shove away her

drink and sit up a little taller, Aggie realized there was more to Emma McDougal Chisholm than she'd thought.

Unless Aggie was losing her touch, the new Mrs. Chisholm had something in her own past she was worried about keeping secret.

Chapter Nine

Halley woke to the wonderful smell of frying bacon and freshly brewed coffee. She quickly showered and dressed before heading downstairs. After making her warm milk, Colton had again checked the entire house to make sure there were no more lethal surprises awaiting her.

He'd tucked her into her bed, kissed her on the forehead and gone downstairs to sleep on her couch. She'd had a devil of a time getting to sleep though, knowing he was just one floor below. But exhaustion had won out and she'd drifted off and slept soundly.

Now as she stepped into the kitchen, she couldn't help but smile. He had on her apron, a frilly thing that had come with the house.

"Nice apron," she said as she leaned into the doorjamb to watch him.

"I went into town and got a few groceries,"

Colton said, smiling at her. "Your refrigerator was sadly bare."

"I smelled the bacon," she said, breathing in the aroma.

"I made cheese omelets to go with it."

She raised a brow in surprise. "So you cook."

He laughed. "I'm just full of surprises."

Wasn't he though.

"Have a seat. Coffee?"

She nodded as she pulled out a chair and sat down, watching him as he poured a mug of coffee and handed it to her. She took a sip and smiled through the steam. "Thank you."

"My pleasure." He filled two plates with bacon, cheese omelet, hash browns and toast. She saw that he'd picked up some huckleberry jam for the toast.

"You thought of everything," she said, impressed. "Thank you again for last night."

He studied her openly for a moment. "Looks like you got some rest."

She touched her wet hair, suddenly self-conscious. She hadn't taken the time to pull it up, so her long hair hung around her shoulders. Her cheeks felt flushed from the shower, from the nearness of this man, and since she didn't have to be at work for a few hours, she'd donned a pair of jeans and a T-shirt. She had taken the time to dab on a little lip gloss, but that was it.

"I looked in on you before I went into town to the store," he said.

Halley felt a small shiver at the thought of him watching her sleep.

"No bad dreams?" he asked.

She shook her head and dug into her breakfast. "This is delicious," she said between bites.

Colton looked pleased as he cleared the dishes, then refilled her coffee mug and took a seat across from her again.

"I didn't want to bring up the Grangers until we'd eaten," he said.

Halley knew they had to talk about the murder investigation and Jessica. But moments before she'd been enjoying the companionable warmth Colton had brought to her kitchen. For a while, she was just a woman, not a deputy, and he was just a man, not the former boyfriend of the deceased, let alone a suspect.

Colton filled her in on his talk with Millie Granger. "I'm telling you her father is involved. Millie practically admitted it."

Halley thought he might be right. But practically admitting it wasn't evidence.

"She admitted he was always overly protective of Jessica, that she was his little girl—"

"None of that is unusual for a father."

Colton swore. "Something was wrong in that house and you know it."

Halley couldn't argue with that. "What are you saying?"

He shook his head, clearly not wanting to say what they were both thinking. The mousy, beaten-down wife, the teenaged promiscuous daughter... As a law enforcement officer, Halley had seen it before.

Halley wished they could have avoided this subject—at least for a little while longer. There was something she needed to ask Colton, but she hated to do it here in her kitchen. She finished her coffee and rose from the table.

"So she wasn't pregnant."

"No." Halley heard relief in his voice. "Apparently, she thought she was and she was upset when she was told that she wasn't."

"So she lied about it and that's probably what got her killed."

Halley didn't miss the irony. If the reason she was killed was because of the baby she said she was carrying, Jessica's lies had finally caught up with her. Colton seemed convinced that that had been the case. Halley was reserving judgment until all the facts were in.

Somewhere in all the lies was the truth, and she'd learned that things were often not as they seemed.

COLTON SAW HALLEY BRACE HERSELF before she said, "I need to know if you were…physical with Jessica, grabbed her a little too roughly, possibly hit her."

So she'd found out about Jessica's bruises. Of course she would suspect him, just as he'd known she would. That was why he hadn't told her.

"Are you asking if we had rough sex?" He let out a humorless laugh as he shoved back the chair and stood. "No. That clear enough for you? I don't expect you to believe me, but I asked Jessica about the bruises because I was concerned that someone was hurting her."

"And what did she say?"

"She got upset, told me to mind my own business. If you must know, it's what we argued about the last time I saw her." He swore. "I didn't tell anyone. I should have, but she'd made it clear that if I did, it was over between us."

He saw sympathy in Halley's gaze. That made him angrier with himself.

"She didn't give you any idea of who might have been hurting her?"

"That's what I'm trying to tell you. It was her old man. Whatever was going on, it was why Jessica was so desperate to get out of that house."

Halley nodded.

He'd expected her to put up an argument and was surprised when she didn't. "You found out something. That's why you aren't telling me how wrong I am."

Halley seemed to hesitate. "Social Services were asked to do a check at the house. It never happened because Jessica disappeared before the social worker got out there. But the doctor did talk to the father. Sid Granger was belligerent and denied touching her in any way."

"Of course he'd say that."

Halley set her mug down on the counter and turned to him, crossing her arms over her chest as she leaned back against the counter. "I'm familiar with the pattern of abuse."

"I doubt it's a coincidence that Jessica was murdered so soon after Social Services and the doctor called about possible physical abuse in the home."

"Looks that way, but we still need proof."

"Sid Granger is guilty as hell and Millie knows it."

"Well, she's either too afraid to talk or she loves her husband and is covering for him. I'm not sure which. Maybe both," Halley said. "I'll see if I can talk to her alone."

"Good luck with that. She had to sneak off to the grocery store to meet me. She was scared to death the entire time, kept looking around as if she expected Sid to appear at any moment."

"In the meantime, steer clear of that family."

EMMA WASN'T SURPRISED to wake the next morning and find her husband gone. Hoyt had come home late. She'd pretended to be asleep, not wanting to have a discussion when they'd both been drinking and were tired.

This morning, after talking to her stepson, Tanner, before he headed off with a load of hay for a neighbor, she'd dressed in jeans, boots and a Western shirt and saddled up and ridden north. She found Hoyt stringing barbed wire with Dawson and Marshall.

Hoyt glanced over as she rode up and did a double take. "You ride?"

She laughed at his shocked expression and thought she couldn't love this man more—even under the circumstances. "There is so much we don't know about each other, isn't there?" She reached into her jacket pocket and handed him his cell phone.

He glanced at it, then at her. His expression changed and he put down the wire stretcher in his hand. "Why don't you boys take it from here. I need to talk to my wife."

Hoyt walked over into the cool shade of the trees where he'd left his horse and, without a word, swung up into the saddle. They rode under a vast Montana morning sky, white clouds bobbing along in all that blue, a cool breeze stirring the silken green branches of the ponderosa pines.

Emma breathed it all in. She refused to believe the strong, handsome, caring and generous man riding beside her was anything but that. Aggie was wrong. Those local women who'd called her were wrong. A woman knew in her heart what a man was really like, didn't she?

They stopped on a high ridge, Hoyt dismounting to reach for her. His large hands cupped her waist as he lifted her from the saddle and lowered her slowly to her feet.

What if you're wrong?

The thought blindsided her. She had followed Hoyt with a trust that, if misguided, could get her killed. With a start she realized that they had ridden far from another living soul. Even if she were to scream, her stepsons wouldn't be able to hear her. At the edge of the high ridge was a precipice that dropped a good twenty feet to a pile of stones. The fall would kill a person.

"Who told you?" Hoyt asked as his gaze met hers.

Emma swallowed. She hated to admit that she'd answered his phone, that she hadn't trusted him. "Aggie."

He let out a curse and stepped away from her to the edge of the rock cliff. "See all of that?" he asked, not turning around. "I own that and it means nothing without you."

She looked out at the land that stretched to the horizon.

"I don't blame you if you want to leave me," he said finally, his voice breaking with emotion.

The sound tore at her heart. She stepped to him, placing a hand on his warm back. "I'm not going anywhere."

He turned then, frowning at her. "That could be the biggest mistake you ever make, Emma."

HALLEY HADN'T SPOKEN TO THE Grangers since her last visit when she'd had to tell them that some remains had been found near the spot where Jessica's purse had been discovered.

Sid had opened the door, making a point of

not asking her in. She'd had to give him the news on his doorstep. He'd been stoic, closing the door after no more than a brief nod and a mumbled, "Thank you for letting us know."

He hadn't asked where the remains had been found. Or if they were absolutely sure that they were his daughter's. Halley hadn't thought it was a good time to ask for a DNA sample. But, still, it was odd that he wouldn't ask where the remains had been found, which led her to believe that he already knew about the secret spot where his daughter had met not only Colton Chisholm—but also at least one other man.

Now, as Halley knocked on the door again, not only did she need to ask for a DNA sample, but she also had to ask about possible abuse of their daughter.

"I can't talk to you," Millie Granger said when she opened the door.

"Mrs. Granger, we have to talk. We can do it here or down at the Sheriff's Department."

Millie had been starting to close the door, but she now stopped. She looked so small and scared, Halley's heart went out to her.

"I want to help you by finding your daughter's killer."

"You can't help me," she whispered and Halley realized that Sid Granger wasn't at work. In fact, he'd been at home the other times Halley had stopped by as well. He suddenly appeared behind his wife.

"I thought you'd be at work," Halley said, caught off guard.

"I'm sure you did," he replied, his mouth twisting into a malicious grin. "I retired so I could spend more time with my wife. Which has been a godsend, given what she's been through. What we've both been through."

Halley suspected that his retirement had less to do with spending time with wife than it did with keeping an eye on her. Why did he feel the need? she wondered. Had he been this possessive of Jessica and, after she was gone, turned that obsession on his wife?

"What do you want now? Haven't you given us enough bad news?" he demanded.

"I need to talk to the two of you," she said, not seeing any other way to handle this at the moment.

"Have you found my daughter's killer?" he asked.

"Not yet."

Sid nodded as if he had expected nothing less, then turned and walked back inside the house.

"Please don't say anything to upset him," Millie whispered as she let Halley into the house.

In the living room, Halley was even more taken aback by the large rattlesnake-skin hide that hung over the fireplace. She thought of the snake in her bed last night. A bite from that kind of rattlesnake wouldn't have killed her, so whoever had left it there for her had been either trying to scare her—or warn her off.

Neither Granger offered her a chair, but she sat down on the couch anyway. It took the couple a few moments to settle into chairs opposite her.

Halley began with the need for a DNA sample.

"What's the point? You're sure it's our daughter, right?" Sid asked.

"We will need positive identification. I thought you would want that as well." He didn't respond, so she continued. "Tell me about your relationship with your daughter," Halley said, taking out her tape recorder. "If you don't mind I'm going to tape our conversation."

Sid eyed it warily. Millie balled her hands in her lap.

"Fine with me," Sid said.

"So did you get along well with your daughter?" Halley asked.

"Jessica was my baby, my sweet girl," he cried. "I loved that girl more than…" His voice broke, tears welling in his eyes.

"She was the only child we were ever going to have," Millie said in her small voice. "We adored her. Didn't we, Sid?"

He nodded. "I would have given her the world. I just can't understand… It was that boy. He ruined my girl. I should have killed him when she told me what he did to her."

"What did Jessica tell you?" Halley asked and saw Millie tense.

Sid worked his jaw, fighting strong emotions, rage among them. "He took my girl's virginity."

"She told you that?"

"Only because I was waiting up for her one night after she'd sneaked out of the house to meet the little bastard. She'd been crying and her dress…" His voice broke again. "It was soiled. There were bruises on her arms. I wanted to go after him right then and there, but Jessica begged me not to. She said…" He swallowed hard. "She said she had wanted him to…" Sid shook his head and clamped his lips together.

"We forbid her to see him again," Millie said. "We thought she'd broken it off…"

Halley looked from one to the other, her gaze finally settling on the father again. "Did you punish Jessica?"

"We grounded her," Millie said.

"You didn't get physical with her?"

"What are you asking?" Sid demanded.

"Jessica had bruises that her doctor noticed when she went in for her checkup about the pregnancy. It appeared that someone had been rough with her."

"It was that boy. She told me he hurt her sometimes," Millie said.

Sid shot his wife a look of disbelief as if this was the first time he'd hear this.

"Colton swears he never harmed her," Halley said.

"*Colton?* You two pretty tight, are you?" Sid sneered at her. "He hurt my girl plenty. He took everything from her—even her life." He was on his feet now. "I think you'd better leave before I say or do something I'll regret. I never touched a hair on my little girl's head. I couldn't even bear it when Millie…" He was crying again.

"I tried to reason with Jessica," Millie said. "And her father did everything possible to get her to come to her senses. No one loved our girl more than Sid."

Halley picked up the tape recorder and shut it off. "Why don't you walk me to the door, Mrs. Granger," she said as rose to leave.

Millie slowly got to her feet, avoiding her husband's scowl.

"I need you to tell me the truth," Halley whispered once they were out on the porch. "Did your husband beat your daughter?"

She seemed to struggle for a moment, before she finally spoke. "It isn't what you think. Jessica had this wild streak. Sid knew it ran on my side of the family. My younger sister went bad. He just didn't want Jessica going down that same path. What he did was for her own good."

"Apparently letting your husband beat your daughter didn't help a lot," Halley said.

"You aren't one to judge. We did the best we could with our baby girl."

"What about the way he treats you? Is that for your own good as well?"

Millie lifted her chin, anger sparking in her eyes. "He's my husband."

"That doesn't give him the right to—"

Sid appeared on the other side of the screen door. "There a problem, deputy?"

"I just wanted to double-check where the two of you were the night Jessica ran away." Halley improvised.

"I believe we already told you that," Sid said, glancing from Halley to his wife, not buying her story.

"It was my quilting night," Millie said. "I

drive down to Old Town Whitehorse to the Whitehorse Sewing Circle."

Sid said, "I was home. As I already told you. Jessica told me she was going to bed. I never knew she was missing until Millie came home and found her bed empty."

Halley turned to Millie. "Why did you happen to check her bed?"

"I went up as I always did to check on her. It's an old habit from when she was a baby."

Sid rubbed his forehead. "I didn't know she'd sneaked out to meet that Colton boy." His jaw tightened again with anger.

The secret meeting spot wasn't that far from the Granger's house. Jessica could have walked along the creek behind her house. Halley wondered how far of a walk it would be—and if there was a path. If Jessica snuck out a lot, there could be.

Jessica had planned to meet Colton at the spot on the creek under the cottonwoods. She'd met Hoyt Chisholm there at 11:30 p.m. and according to him seemed to be waiting around, as if expecting someone else.

Colton wasn't supposed to be there until midnight.

Was it possible that she was meeting someone else first?

The question was—who?

And the bigger question: Did her father follow her that night?

Chapter Ten

Halley had barely gotten back to the Sheriff's Department to type up her report when Colton called.

"I've been thinking about this morning," he said.

She thought of her kitchen, the wonderful smell of coffee and bacon, and Colton in the apron making her breakfast, and smiled to herself.

"It's possible there might have been someone Jessica confided in—other than her friend Twyla," he said.

So that's what Colton had been thinking about. Not this morning in her kitchen. She thought about that moment when they'd both left the house this morning. Colton had hesitated. She'd seen something simmer in his gaze.

They'd been standing just inches apart. She'd

been so sure he was going to kiss her again that she'd almost leaned in.

"See you later?" he'd said and stepped back, as if needing to put distance between them.

She'd nodded dumbly, wondering about this overly gentlemanly Colton Chisholm. He hadn't tried anything last night and then this morning... "Later," she'd managed to say as he'd walked to his pickup.

Now mentally shifting gears, she asked, "You have an idea who that might have been?"

"Possibly. I saw her once after school talking to our guidance counselor."

"The married, older man?"

"He was married and he was probably ten years older than us."

She knew Colton must have seen something between Jessica and the guidance counselor years ago that had made him suspicious.

"He is still at the school," Colton said. "There is something else I should tell you. If he is the older, married man Jessica told me about, then he might have taken photographs of the two of them together."

Halley could hear how angry he was and couldn't help being surprised Colton hadn't pulled his cowboy- on-a-big-white-horse routine and already confronted the man. She said as much to him.

"I thought about it," he said with a humorless laugh. "Believe me, I wanted to go over to his house and… But I realized I had to let you handle this investigation."

He was finally trusting her to find Jessica's killer. Her heart swelled at the compliment. "Thank you. For telling me about the guidance counselor and for not going over there yourself," she added.

"Let me know what happens?" he asked.

She was still touched by his faith in her. "What's this man's name?"

"Mark Jensen."

THE BREEZE SIGHED IN the ponderosa pines. Nearby the horses ambled off to eat the tall green grass growing along the ridgeline.

"Emma, I should never have married you."

She stared at her husband, all her fears coming home to roost in those few words from his lips. She stumbled back from the edge of the cliff, suddenly needing to sit down. Lowering herself onto a lichen-covered rock, she felt a little better.

Hoyt sat down next to her. "I should have told you everything from the very beginning, but I knew once I did…" His gaze softened as he looked at her. "Aggie Wells has been calling me. I was going to tell you. I just didn't know how."

Emma saw the man she'd fallen so desperately in love with. "I know you didn't have anything to do with your wives' deaths or disappearance."

He chuckled. "Oh, Emma, it is that faith in me and your love that made me throw caution to the wind and marry you."

"You definitely have had bad luck when it comes to wives," she said.

He smiled at her. "Until now."

"You should have trusted me."

"You have no idea how difficult it was for me to even ask you out—let alone marry you. It still scares the hell out of me."

"Tell me you don't believe in some stupid curse."

"What else could it be?" he said.

"Bad luck? Or perhaps you married the wrong women."

He laughed, but there was no humor in it. "My first wife, Laura, I met at a college back East. She said she always wanted to live on a ranch and have a dozen children. When we found out she couldn't have children of our own, I suggested adopting. She had seemed so happy to get the three boys…" His voice died off for a moment. "They were just babies. I swear I didn't know she was leaving me—not until I got the divorce papers two days after she drowned. The boat trip on Fort Peck Reservoir was her idea. She said she needed a break from the boys."

"How did she drown?"

"We got caught in a storm. Fort Peck can be dangerous when the wind comes up. The boat capsized. When I surfaced, I couldn't find her. I dived time and again…" He looked away.

Emma could see how that could make an insurance company nervous. "You had a life insurance policy on her that paid double indemnity."

Hoyt turned to meet her gaze. "And I asked to take an insurance policy out on you as well." He let out another harsh laugh. "I told you it's because of the business, but we won't go through with it if it makes you feel better."

She shook her head, although she suspected that there was more to the story about Laura that Hoyt didn't want to tell her. Had they fought? Is that what had capsized the boat? Or had it really been the storm?

"Tell me about your second wife."

"Tasha was from California. She was up here on a dinosaur dig and she had this idea that living on a ranch would be romantic. By then

I had adopted three more sons who needed homes."

"You had six boys to raise," Emma said. "I can see where you would want another wife."

"Tasha said she couldn't have kids of her own and had seemed delighted to suddenly have six sons." His expression grew sad. "She had gone for a horseback ride alone even though I'd asked her not to until she'd spent more time on a horse. I found her. She'd somehow gotten her boot caught in the stirrup. She'd been dragged to death."

"Hoyt, I'm so sorry."

"I wasn't going to remarry, but a young woman named Krystal had been working at the house, helping Tasha... The boys had taken a shine to her. She had a boyfriend in Wyoming who was trying to get her back... I just couldn't bear for the boys to lose another person they cared about."

"So you married her," Emma said. "And she disappeared. Are you sure she just didn't go back to her old boyfriend?"

Hoyt shrugged.

"And then Aggie came back into your life and after seven years you had Krystal declared dead."

He nodded. "I swore I wasn't getting married

again." He hung his head looking embarrassed. "For years I raised the boys alone."

Emma decided this wasn't the time to remind him that they were no longer boys.

"Hoyt, oh, honey." She moved to kneel at his feet and wrap her arms around him. "That's so horrible. No wonder you were afraid to love again."

"Aggie Wells is convinced that I killed all three of them."

"I know. She just doesn't realize the kind of man you really are. But she will, I promise."

He drew back. "Emma, what have you done?"

BEFORE THEY HUNG UP, Colton asked if Halley had talked to Millie Granger.

"I just got back from her house. I tried to talk to her but Sid was there. She is definitely frightened of him."

Colton swore. "I still think Sid killed Jessica. I suppose it's possible that if Millie starts to believe that he killed their daughter to keep the truth from coming out about the physical abuse, then maybe she will come forward."

"Maybe," Halley said. "In the meantime, it would help if Jessica confided in someone about what was going on at home."

"I suppose she could have confided in the guidance counselor even if she was sleeping with him." Colton sounded skeptical.

"We don't even know for a fact that any of what Jessica told you was true," she pointed out. "So tell me about this counselor."

"Mark Jensen was in his late twenties, so he'd be forty or so by now, a good-looking guy that everyone liked."

"Especially Jessica?"

"Yeah. The one time I saw her with him, he was very attentive and Jessica…she was flirting with him." He let out a humorless, self-deprecating laugh. "Twyla asked me why I never saw it."

"Because you didn't want to," Halley said.

"Yeah."

"Love does strange things to people."

"I'm not so sure that was love," Colton said. "I felt she needed me. She…hell, who knows what she wanted from me."

Halley thought about the first time she'd fallen in love. At least it had felt like true love. She could still remember the pain of seeing Colton with Jessica and realizing that he wouldn't be tormenting her anymore. Amazing that it could still hurt even after all these years.

MARK JENSEN LOOKED UP expectantly as Halley tapped on his open door. Something passed over his expression that could have been worry as he took in her uniform shirt and the gun at her hip. She had called his house and been told by his wife that Mark was at his office at the school even though it was a Saturday.

"Mr. Jensen?" she asked.

Mark nodded a little too eagerly. "Yes."

"Do you have a minute?"

He glanced at his desk as if hoping he could find something important there so he could say no. Apparently finding nothing, he said, "Of course." He motioned her into his small office where she sat on a plastic chair across from his desk.

Since it was Saturday, the high school had a hollow, empty feel about it. She had seen only one other person as she'd walked through the building, a janitor. He'd directed her to the counselor's office.

Mark Jensen *was* a good-looking man, just as Colton had said. She'd had a couple of high school teachers she'd had crushes on and could remember that little thrill she'd gotten when one of them had complimented her on a paper or given her a smile after she'd answered a question correctly.

"I'm Deputy Robinson."

Halley noticed that Mark Jensen didn't look at her. "So what can I do for you?"

"I'm here about Jessica Granger. You might have heard—"

"Yes, terrible. I'm shocked."

"You remember her then?"

"Of course."

Halley pulled out her tape recorder from her purse and turned it on. "If you don't mind, Mr. Jensen, I'm going to tape this. It's standard procedure."

He picked up a pen from the desk and started playing with it nervously. "Sure. Whatever."

"What was your relationship with Jessica Granger?"

He looked uncomfortable. "I was her guidance counselor."

"Did she confide in you?" Halley asked.

"About what?"

"About her boyfriend problems, school problems, problems at home." She saw that she'd hit on something. "She told you about her trouble with her father?"

"She mentioned that he was too rough on her."

"*Rough* on her?"

"You know, too strict."

"You knew it was more than that."

He hesitated a moment then nodded slowly. "One day after class I noticed a bruise on her arm and asked her about it. She told me her father beat her and begged me not to say anything to anyone because it would only make things worse for her and her mother." He looked rueful. "I should have reported it, but I really worried that she was right. Even if Social Services got her out of there, her mother would still be in the house. Jessica said her mother would never leave her father. You don't think…"

"We're looking at all suspects," Halley assured him.

"I met Sid Granger only once. The man had a scary temper," Mark said.

"Jessica confided in you about running away, didn't she?" Halley asked.

Mark looked hesitant. "Yes, she told me."

"You and Jessica must have been close for her to confide in you."

"No more than any other student," Mark said quickly. He was flustered now.

"Mr. Jensen, I have to ask you if you slept with Jessica."

The counselor leaned back in his chair, dropping the pen to the floor. For a moment, she could see that he had thought about reaching down to pick it up, but changed his mind. "I'm not sure what you've been told…" he said, his eyes darting back and forth. "But I can assure you—"

"Did you believe you were the father of her baby?"

The counselor shot to his feet. "I'm going to have to ask you to leave."

"Jessica said the older, married man she was sleeping with kept photos of the two of them," Halley said. "I need to take a look in your desk drawers, Mr. Jensen."

"Just a minute. I know my rights."

She pulled out her phone.

"Who are you calling?" the counselor asked, sounding even more upset.

"A judge, to issue me a warrant to search your office. In the meantime, I'm afraid I'm going to have to read you your rights and take you into custody. Anything you say…"

Mark Jensen looked defeated as he slowly dropped back into his desk chair. There were tears in his eyes as he said, "I knew that girl would destroy me. You have no idea what she was like."

"I know she was underage, a good ten years younger than you were," Halley said.

He let out a bark of a laugh. "She seduced *me*. I was a babe in the woods compared to her."

"So you thought it was your baby," Halley said. "Jessica made demands on you?"

"She wanted me to run away with her. Just quit my job, leave my family, take off. And you know the worst part? I was tempted."

"Is that why you killed her, Mr. Jensen?"

"I want a lawyer," he said. "I'm not saying another word until I see a lawyer."

"You might be interested to know that Jessica Granger wasn't pregnant," Halley said.

He swore. "That lying bitch. I gave her $500 to get an abortion."

"When was that?"

He shook his head.

"Was it the night she disappeared?" Halley asked.

"A week before," Mark said.

Halley wondered if some of that cash was the $200 found in her purse. "But you saw her the night she was running away, didn't you, Mr. Jensen?"

"I told you. I need to talk to a lawyer. *Now*."

Later, after a deputy delivered the warrant, Halley got the janitor to break into the locked bottom drawer of Mark Jensen's desk.

She already knew what she was going to find. Still, some of the photographs came as a shock.

COLTON KNEW HE SHOULD be relieved after Halley's call. It appeared that Jessica's murderer had been caught. Mark Jensen hadn't broken down and confessed, but he might if his alibi didn't check out—and Halley managed to find the $10,000 that had disappeared that night.

The whole thing still felt like a nightmare. Colton couldn't believe the things he'd learned about Jessica or the fact that she was dead. Murdered.

Mark Jensen was guilty as hell—if not of murder then of having sex with a student. What had made him keep the photographs after all this time? No doubt because Jessica had that kind of hold over the man. Jensen hadn't forgotten her, couldn't.

Sid Granger was guilty as well. Even if he didn't kill his daughter, he had physically abused her. He was the reason she was running away. It bothered Colton that Sid might get off scot-free when he was at least partially to blame for Jessica's death.

Colton knew that Jessica had brought a lot of this on herself. But what had made her the way she was? Had it been some wild streak in her that even Sid Granger couldn't beat out of her? Or had it been his overprotectiveness that had pushed her to rebel in such a way? Colton would never know.

Colton was waiting for Halley when she came out of the Sheriff's Department that afternoon. He admired the way she'd handled herself. She made a damn good deputy. She was tough and yet all woman. He wished things had been different years ago.

"Could we have dinner or something later?" he asked impulsively.

Halley quirked a brow at him.

"Yeah, Halley, I'm asking you out on a date. You do date, don't you?"

"Yes." She sounded defensive.

He grinned. "When was your last date?"

"When was *yours?*" she shot back. Then she added, "Okay, you got me there. But I still don't think that's such a good idea. This is an ongoing investigation and—"

"Seven? I'll pick you up. Wear something sexy." He climbed back into the pickup before she could argue. He'd just driven away when his cell phone rang. It was Emma.

"I wanted to make sure you were at supper tonight," she said.

"I have a date," he said.

"A *date?*"

"Don't sound so surprised."

"Mind if I ask who this date is with?"

"Halley." He heard the pleasure in the small sound she made. "Wasn't that what you were hoping?"

"I don't know what you're talking about. We'll miss you at supper." She hung up, amusement in her voice.

He snapped his phone shut, realizing that he hadn't asked why she wanted to make sure everyone was at supper. Another surprise guest?

Feeling lost, he drove toward his place outside of Whitehorse. It was a small house, a two-story, much like the one Halley was renting. Like her, he hadn't done much to make the house a home. Living there had always felt temporary, as if he was just waiting for his life to start. Is that how Halley felt as well?

He couldn't help but think about this morning. He'd come so close to kissing her. Last night he had lain awake for hours on the couch, unable to sleep knowing she was just one floor above him. He'd wanted to go to her, but he hadn't. He didn't want to ruin things with her this time, so he was forcing himself to take things slow. He smiled as he thought about their date tonight.

Somehow, he had to make it perfect.

HALLEY WAS FEELING GOOD except that she was running late for her date. She had Mark Jensen behind bars. She still hadn't been able to verify his alibi, but he'd been charged with numerous felonies and wasn't going anywhere.

Mostly she was excited about her date tonight with Colton. She was practically giddy and chastised herself for being so silly. It was just a date. With Colton Chisholm!

She grinned as she climbed out of her patrol SUV and carried the small bags of groceries she'd picked up at the store. She'd been embarrassed that she'd had so little in her refrigerator last night.

As she started toward the house, she noticed the dark clouds that had moved in. It surprised her—and gave her a strange chill of apprehension. Halley didn't believe in omens, but if she had, this ominous sky certainly would have worried her.

The air felt heavy. Black clouds covered the sun, dropping like a blanket over the landscape. Pockets of deep shadows hunkered around the house as the wind whipped the trees, sending leaves flying through the air.

"So you really are renting this dump."

Halley dropped the two bags of groceries at her feet as Sid Granger stepped from the shadows of the sagging porch. Too late she saw his vehicle parked in the cloudy darkness beside the old barn out back. She realized it was no accident that he'd parked back there. He'd wanted to surprise her. He'd been lying in wait for her.

Chapter Eleven

"Little jumpy, aren't you?" Sid Granger asked, amusement and something more sinister in his voice, as he stepped from the shadows beside Halley's house.

Her hand dropped to the weapon still strapped to her hip. Her heart rate leaped, first out of surprise, then as she got a good look at him. He barely resembled the man she'd seen at his house earlier. His hair was disheveled, his clothes dirty. She could smell the alcohol on him as he staggered into the pale yellow of the ranch yard light that automatically came on as the storm moved in. He had a can of beer in his hand, and it clearly hadn't been his first.

But it was the look in his eyes that made her unsnap the loop on her holster and settle her hand over the grip.

"Mr. Granger, what are you doing here?"

"There a law against it?" He drained the last swallow of beer, tilting the can up and almost falling over backward. Then he crushed the can in his large, pawlike hands and leveled his gaze at her. "Colton Chisholm needs to pay for what he did to my little girl. I want to know what you're going to do about it."

Halley wasn't about to come to Colton's defense. Not here. Not with a man as drunk and angry as Sid Granger. He was looking for a fight, but he wasn't going to find it with her.

She eased her hand off the weapon at her side, bent down and, never letting him out of her sight, picked up the groceries she'd dropped. "It's late and I haven't had my dinner. I'm mean when I haven't eaten." She started to step past him.

He grabbed her arm, squeezing her flesh painfully as he jerked her toward him. She smelled sweat and beer and an uncontrolled anger that she suspected was always just below the surface.

"I asked you a question," he bellowed, tightening his hold. "I saw how it was between you and *Colton*. You think I don't know about women like you? I had a daughter just like you. An alley cat who'd sleep with any big tom that came around. I learned the hard way how to handle a woman like you."

"And how is that?" Halley asked. His fingers dug into her flesh, making her wince.

So he had known about Jessica's promiscuity and he'd just said he'd known how to handle a woman like that.

Sid Granger's gaze narrowed to tiny slits, reminding her of the rattlesnake she'd found in her bed.

When he didn't answer her, she said, "Bully them? Beat them? Put rattlesnakes in their beds? Is that how you handled it, Mr. Granger?"

He released her so quickly, it caught her by surprise. She stumbled back.

One of the grocery bags slipped from her grasp and fell to the ground again.

"What the hell did you just say?" he demanded.

She could see the confusion and what could have been shock on his face, yet she didn't believe it. "I saw the rattlesnake on your wall. I know you put one in my bed. Don't bother to deny it. Just as I know you beat your daughter, and your wife stood by and let you."

His shock was replaced by a sadness so deep that his features seemed to dissolve in the storm light. "My baby girl. My poor baby girl. It's something in their blood. It makes them the way they are. Not their fault." The first drops of rain came out of the dark clouds like bullets. They smacked the old farmhouse's roof, ricocheted off the patrol car and pelted the two of them and the bags of groceries, one on the ground, the other dangling from Halley's fingers.

Over the racket she heard the sound of a vehicle coming and swore. Her date was early and she was running even later, thanks to Sid Granger.

He seemed to stir, as if seeing her for the first time. Suddenly he clamped a hand over his mouth as if he was going to be sick and spun away, half loping, half stumbling to his vehicle parked by the barn.

She watched him go as the clouds seemed to burst open and huge raindrops pelted down on her. She stood wondering if she had the wrong man behind bars for Jessica's murder as she heard a pickup turn into her drive. Colton was early—and she was worse than just not ready for what she feared might be the most important date of her life.

AGGIE WELLS HAD BEEN to the Chisholm ranch house before—just as Emma had suspected. But as she parked in front of the big, rambling house, she was still impressed. It was two stories, sprawling across what appeared to be a half acre of lawn. A wide porch ran across the front. The chairs and rockers all looked well-worn with a history that she envied.

"You are too emotionally involved in these cases," her boss had told her when he'd tried to take her off the Chisholm case.

"He killed those women," she'd argued, making him shake his head. "I'm getting the insurance company's money back."

"No, Aggie, you're not. You've gone beyond investigating this man. It's become an obsession. You're out of control, breaking laws, doing God only knows what to prove you're right."

She didn't deny that she broke the insurance companies rules and even a few laws. But visiting the Chisholm house when everyone was gone wasn't exactly breaking and entering. They left their door unlocked. Anyone could have walked in—and did.

She'd looked through thc whole place, getting a feel for what it would be like to live there with a man like Hoyt Chisholm—and trying to learn everything she could about his new wife, Emma.

Aggie had known Hoyt would marry again. It was his pattern. His first wife had been close to his age, but the second two had been younger. Aggie had expected number four to be young as well and had been surprised to find Emma closer to Hoyt's own age—hers as well.

A change in his pattern? And just when she thought she had him figured out. So what was it about Emma? Aggie was looking forward to seeing the two of them together so she could judge for herself why Hoyt Chisholm had dared marry again—and to a woman nothing like the others.

She studied the house, worried that she was missing something important about this change in pattern, then, giving up, she opened her car door and stepped out into the fading light.

Storm clouds crowded the horizon. Wind howled at the eaves of the house and sent dust devils spinning across the yard.

Aggie frowned as she thought about the woman she'd met at the bar. Emma was stronger, more determined and definitely feistier than the others. Aggie had liked her and, from what she'd gathered during her in-house investigation, Hoyt was wild about her. At least for the moment.

She'd especially taken her time in the master bedroom and had searched it thoroughly, intrigued by the woman even before she'd met Emma.

With a chill, she remembered that the bed hadn't been made yet, the covers thrown back, the sheets in a tangle. She had stood there imagining the two of them in that bed. It had made her sick to think of how it would all end.

As it began to rain, she hurried toward the house, thinking again of the argument she'd had with her boss.

"Aggie, I don't understand what's happened to you. You used to be one of my best investigators. Then you took the first Chisholm case and something happened to you. It's almost as if—like his wives—you've fallen under his spell. Almost as if you've fallen in love with Hoyt Chisholm."

She grimaced now at how ridiculous her boss's accusations had been. This was about simple justice.

No, she amended as Emma Chisholm stepped out onto the porch to greet her. There was nothing simple about this. Emma Chisholm was going to die and she didn't even realize it yet.

THROUGH THE POURING RAIN, Colton saw Halley in front of her house picking up a bag of groceries from the ground, a strange expression on her face. In a flash of lightning, he saw a vehicle come careening around the side of the house, Sid Granger's stark face illuminated behind the wheel.

He jumped out of the truck, having put on his slicker before leaving his house when he saw the thunderstorm to the south, and ran toward Halley. "Did that bastard do something to you?"

She shook her head, her hair wet and clinging to her face. She looked like she might cry.

"If he hurt you—"

"I'm sorry. I'm not ready for our date. I was running late. I…"

He stared at her through the rain as thunder and lightning filled the sky around them. "That's why you're upset?"

She nodded and he laughed as he took the groceries from her and said, "Then I guess we'd better get you inside."

He was going to say "and get out of those wet clothes," but the words caught in his throat as she looked up at him with those big brown eyes. Desire shot through him. He was no longer aware of the drowning rain or the lightning or the thunder that boomed so close it made the hair on the back of his neck stand up.

"We really should go inside," he said, his voice sounding strange, even to him.

He carried her groceries into the house, Halley trailing him into the kitchen, both of them leaving puddles on the floor. He heard her on her cell phone and realized she was calling the Sheriff's Department to have Sid Granger picked up.

He put the groceries on the counter and turned as she hung up. "You said he didn't hurt you." He stepped to her, gently touching her upper arm where bruises were already beginning to darken the skin.

"He grabbed me, but I'm all right. I had to put in a call to have him picked up. He's drunk and in no condition to be driving. I don't want him killing someone on his way home."

"Or taking it out on his wife?"

She nodded.

Colton stood inches from her, afraid of what Sid had done. "Something happened that has you upset. Something more than not being ready for our date."

Halley shook her head. "I'm not sure what happened. Sid had been waiting for me. He didn't exactly threaten me… But he did scare me and that made me angry. I mentioned the snake he put in my bed and he kind of freaked."

"He must have been surprised that you knew it was him."

"Maybe." She shivered.

"You really need to get out of those wet clothes." He turned away as he said it this time. "I'll put your groceries away while you change for our date." He hesitated, considering the items he saw in the grocery bags. Two steaks, a small bag of potatoes, sour cream, butter, asparagus and a bottle of wine.

Had she been thinking they would stay here for dinner? The idea sent a wave of desire through him. "Unless you want to..." When he turned back around, there was a small puddle on the kitchen floor where she'd been standing, but no Halley.

A moment later he heard the sound of the shower running upstairs.

As EMMA WATCHED AGGIE during dinner, she thought maybe the woman was beginning to see that Hoyt wasn't the dangerous man she thought he was.

"This beef is delicious," Aggie had said, looking from Emma to Hoyt. "Did you raise it?"

He'd actually smiled as he answered that he had. At first he had been tense, but he'd relaxed as the dinner had progressed. Even her stepsons were on their best behavior and she could tell that Aggie was enjoying herself.

Emma was beginning to think she might have a knack for bringing people together. After all, Colton had a date with Halley tonight.

She smiled to herself as she listened to Aggie visiting with Hoyt. He'd been so sure that this had been a terrible idea. Emma had a theory that often when enemies were forced to sit down together over a meal, they came to see the other person differently. It humanized their enemy and made it harder to hate them.

"Emma, you are an amazing cook," Aggie said, turning to smile over at her.

"Thank you, but I had help."

"Don't let her kid you," Hoyt spoke up, then lowered his voice to add, "she's the one who turns out the great food from that kitchen. She is a woman of many talents."

Emma basked in his praise—and the sensual look he gave her. When she glanced at Aggie again, she caught her frowning. The woman quickly changed her expression but was quieter through dessert.

When supper was over, Emma walked her to the porch.

A warm summer rain fell in a dark sheet at the edge of the porch steps. Emma loved the sound, but felt a chill as Aggie came to stand beside her.

"Thank you for a wonderful meal and a very interesting evening," Aggie said, glancing back at the house. "You really seem to have turned this household around." She quickly added, "Hoyt said you make his boys dress for dinner—no cow manure on their boots, hands washed and even a prayer before they're allowed to eat."

"Just common courtesy where I'm from."

"And where is that, Emma?" Aggie's eyes had narrowed, and she was openly studying her.

Emma laughed. "It's enough that you're intent on investigating my husband. Do you still believe he killed all three of his former wives?" she asked pointedly.

"I have to admit, seeing him in his natural habitat does make me wonder," Aggie admitted. "But his last three wives are dead. I would think you're the one who should be worrying about that."

"I believe his third wife is still missing," she pointed out for the second time. "Unless you know something I don't."

Aggie prepared to run through the rain to her car. "You really are something. If one of his wives can survive being married to him, it just might be you, Emma. But I wouldn't count on it. At least you've been warned."

"I appreciate your concern, but I'm not going to let it keep me up at night," she said.

"Oh, did I mention there was a witness on the lake the day his first wife died?" Aggie asked.

Emma felt her heart drop.

"The fisherman was too far away to hear what was being said, but he saw them both standing up in the boat as if they were arguing right before the boat capsized and no one ever saw Laura Chisholm again. It's just something to think about as you're about to fall asleep."

With that the investigator ran to her car.

HALLEY TOOK A QUICK SHOWER to warm up. She was still shaken by Sid Granger's strange visit—and the reminder of who was waiting for her downstairs. As she stepped out, she heard thunder, then a crack of lightning so close she flinched. She quickly toweled dry, not wanting to keep Colton waiting.

She'd thought about offering to make them dinner here at the house and had bought everything she needed. Going out with him under the circumstances didn't seem like a wise thing to do—especially after Sid Granger's visit.

In front of her closet, she stared at the few dressy clothes she owned. Five days a week she wore a uniform. On the weekends, she wore jeans and a T-shirt. She'd never had a good reason to dress up other than for a friend's wedding. The few men she'd dated took her fishing or canoeing or to a movie or bowling.

Colton had told her to wear something sexy. Sure.

Halley dug through her closet and found one little red print sundress. It was simple and not what she would call sexy. But it would have to do.

She slipped it over her head. The lightweight silken fabric dropped over her, settling on her curves. In her vanity mirror, she saw that her cheeks were fired with heat from her shower.

"You all right up there?" Colton called from the foot of the stairs.

"I'll be right down!" She dabbed a little lip gloss on, noting that her eyes looked overly bright. Fighting to still her excitement as well as her anxiety, she straightened and ran a brush through her thick mane of burnished hair. It fell around her shoulders in a dark wave, contrasting with the red of the dress and her slightly tanned arms and legs.

Feeling like Cinderella going to the ball, she slipped into her only pair of dress sandals and went downstairs.

Colton was waiting for her in the living room. He'd been standing at the window, looking out at the downpour, but he turned the moment he heard her approach.

Even in the dim light from the storm, she saw his eyes light up at the sight of her. "Great dress," he said and let out a low whistle.

She had to bite her tongue not to say, "Oh, this old thing?" Instead she stood feeling self-conscious and shy.

"We're going to have to make a run for my pickup," he said as he stepped toward her. "I'm sorry I picked a lousy night for our date."

"It's not your fault a thunderstorm blew in." She met his gaze and felt a jolt. If he kept looking at her like that—

"We should go. I don't want to be late for our dinner reservation," he said, but didn't move.

Her heart began to pound harder, and she knew even before he lowered his mouth toward hers that he was going to kiss her.

Her pulse kicked up a beat as his lips touched hers. The kiss beside the road the other day had been quick and impulsive. This kiss was a keeper, slow and sensual.

It stole her breath. She leaned into him as he deepened the kiss. It felt so wonderful being in his arms. The thunderstorm boomed around them, but Halley felt as if she was in a warm cocoon. Desire spiked through her as hot and bright as the lightning outside the window. Her pulse pounded like the rain on the roof, her heart booming as loudly as the thunder.

COLTON DREW BACK FROM the kiss feeling as if one of those bolts of lightning had just struck him. He shook his head. He'd never wanted a woman the way he wanted Halley Robinson at this moment, but he'd be damned. He was taking her on a *date*. He wasn't carrying her upstairs right now and making love to her...

"We need to go," he said, his voice sounding strained.

Halley nodded, looking uncomfortable. Was she as disappointed as he was? He'd seen desire in her dark eyes. The same desire he'd seen the first time he'd kissed her.

"I'll get my jacket," she said, sounding as breathless as he felt.

They were soaked to the skin by the time they reached his pickup. Both of them had seemed at a loss for words as he started the truck and headed up the road toward the county highway. He'd wanted this date to be perfect, dammit, and nothing was going as he'd planned it.

Rain fell hard and fast. Every low spot on the road had filled with water. The dirt underneath was now slick mud. He felt the tires spin out and shifted into four-wheel drive. Not that it helped much, since in this part of the country the mud was known as gumbo, making a lot of roads impassible—this might be one of them.

He had gone less than a quarter mile up the road when, after busting through a deep puddle, the back of the pickup fishtailed around. He tried to regain control but on the slick mud, there was no way. The truck slid into the ditch and, even though he tried, he knew it was stuck until the road dried out. He doubted that even a tow truck could get him out tonight.

Colton swore. Nothing about this date was going right. When he looked over at Halley, he saw tears in her eyes. "I'm sorry. I wanted this date to be perfect and…" He unsnapped his seat belt and slid over to take her in his arms. "I wanted to do everything right, take it slow, not mess up with you again."

She smiled through her tears. "I think it's perfect," she said as her gaze locked with his.

He laughed softly as he brushed a lock of wet hair off her cheek. "Then I wouldn't change a thing."

Chapter Twelve

The day dawned warm and dry and beautiful, the storm forgotten except for the fresh smell the rain had left over the land.

Halley woke to see Colton propped up on one elbow lying beside her in her bed, smiling down at her. They were both still clothed and under the comforter he'd thrown over them late last night.

"I want to take you out to dinner tonight," he said. "A real date."

She chuckled at that as he bent to kiss her. They had stayed in the warm cab of the pickup, kissing and talking until the rain had let up a little. Then they'd made a run for the house. By the time they'd reached the front porch, they were both soaked and muddy from slipping and sliding that had ultimately resulted in a spill that took them both down in the warm mud.

Halley smiled to herself, remembering her

first date with Colton Chisholm. It hadn't been that much different from the old days, except that there hadn't been fighting when they ended up wrestling in the mud.

After a hot shower and a change of clothing, he'd cooked the food she'd brought home. They hadn't made love.

"Sorry," he'd said as he'd covered his eyes and handed her a towel after their shower. "I don't make love on the first date."

Colton had proved that it wasn't just breakfast he excelled in cooking. They'd eaten their steaks, baked potatoes and buttered asparagus at her kitchen table as the storm raged around them. They'd laughed and visited as if they'd known each other their whole lives. In a way, they had.

Then they'd gone back upstairs and laid down on the bed, talking and kissing until they'd fallen asleep, holding each other.

Halley glanced at the clock. "I have to get to work. If I can get out to the county road."

"You should be able to make it if you go off road through the grass. I'll get one of my brothers to come over with a tractor and pull out my pickup. I think it has dried enough for us to get it out. So do I get to take you out tonight on a real date?"

"I liked our date last night," she said, leaning in to kiss him again.

"Me, too."

She started to tell him that she still didn't think their being seen together was a good idea right now, but he stopped her.

"Are you worried that you don't have the killer behind bars?"

"No." Right now both Mark Jensen and Sid Granger were behind bars. Last night she'd gotten a call from one of the other deputies that they'd picked up Sid and charged him with driving under the influence. He would have to go before a judge before he could get out of jail.

"I have to get going." She slipped out of bed and headed for the shower. A moment later she heard him outside the bathroom door.

"I'll call you later," he said. "Halley? I had a really good time last night."

She smiled. "I did, too."

COLTON HEARD ABOUT LAST night's supper at the ranch from his stepbrothers.

"I kid you not, the woman is a private investigator for an insurance company and from what I gathered, she's *investigating* Dad," Marshall said.

"For what?" Colton asked, although he

suspected that he knew. He and his brothers had been too young to hear any talk when Laura Chisholm had drowned. When Tasha died, there was talk. It wasn't until Krystal disappeared that Colton had heard the rumors about his father.

He'd ignored them and so had his brothers. There were always rumors circulating around Whitehorse—especially if your name was Chisholm.

"So Dad's had bad luck with wives," he said and looked to his brothers for agreement. They had gathered out by the corrals—out of earshot of the house and Emma and their father.

"Three dead wives is more than bad luck," Marshall said.

"We don't know that Krystal is dead," Zane spoke up.

"Dad had her legally declared dead," Tanner reminded them.

"That doesn't mean—"

Colton cut off Logan. "Dad had nothing to do with their deaths."

"We know that," Dawson agreed. "But that isn't what that investigator believes. I was watching her at dinner. She hardly took her eyes off Dad. She's trouble. I remember the last time she came around. I thought I saw her coming out of the house. I told Dad, but he said I had to be mistaken. I wasn't."

The brothers stood looking at each other.

"I'll see what I can find out about her," Colton said.

HALLEY HAD FORGOTTEN THAT she'd left a message for Hazel Rimes to call her. When her cell phone rang later that afternoon, it took her a moment to remember who Hazel Rimes even was.

"I'm sorry," the elderly woman apologized for not getting back to the deputy sooner. "I was over in Great Falls, visiting my daughter and that bunch of wild animals she calls her kids." Hazel laughed. "I love them all, but it sure is nice to be home. But that probably isn't why you called me, to hear about my grandkids."

"No." Not that it probably mattered anymore. "I was just curious about the letter you found at the post office, the one that had fallen between the wall and counter."

"The letter to Colton Chisholm? *I* didn't find it," Hazel said. "I was just the one who handed it to Nell. No, let me think. Oh, yes, I remember, it was Millie Granger. She's the one who spotted it. I'd have never seen it. Only a little corner of the envelope was sticking out. It's a wonder anyone noticed at all. I guess Millie did because she was standing right there by the counter."

Halley felt her heart beat a little faster. "But she asked you to get it and give it to Nell?"

"That's right. Nell had gone back to get a package for me."

"Was anyone else there in the lobby with you and Millie?"

"Not that I remember. Oh, I can't swear there wasn't. My memory isn't all that great. You could ask Millie. She's sharper than me," she added with a laugh. "I'd have never seen that letter and it would still be there another fourteen years."

"I'm just confused about why Millie would ask you to retrieve the letter if she was right there."

"She said, 'You get it. I just had my nails done.' I didn't mind. Was there a problem with the letter?"

"No, I was just curious. So you both looked at it before giving it to Nell?"

"We were just shocked when we saw the postmark, let alone who it was from," Hazel was saying. "Millie had to remind me that her daughter had dated Colton Chisholm. Frankly, I barely remembered Jessica. She always seemed like such a shy, retiring girl. Kinda skittish, you know?"

Something like that. "Well, thank you for calling me back, and welcome home."

"It's good to be here. That's a long drive from Great Falls. I did stop in Havre for a bite to eat."

Halley was no longer listening. Her heart drummed in her chest. Millie Granger was the one who found the letter from her daughter? Given the way she and Sid felt about Colton, there is no way she would have let that letter be delivered, was there?

Unless the postmistress had come back in and Millie had felt she had no choice.

Hazel finally quit talking and Halley was able to hang up. That lost letter had bothered her from the start. She had to pull over to the side of the road, her hands were shaking so hard and her head was spinning.

When her cell phone rang again, she thought it was Hazel calling her back for some reason or other. It was Colton.

"I need to ask a favor," he said.

"Sure."

"Would you see what you can find out about a woman named Agatha Wells. She's an investigator for Royalty Life Insurance Company."

Halley wanted to ask why he needed the information, but he didn't give her a chance.

"What time should I pick you up for our date?"

She glanced at her watch. "Why don't you make it eight? I have something I need to do before I head home."

"Is everything all right?"

"It will be once I check on something," she told him.

COLTON COULDN'T SIT STILL. He was anxious to hear what Halley had found out about the insurance investigator and excited about their date tonight. He had time to kill before he picked her up.

He felt badly that he hadn't worked at the ranch in days. His brothers were moving cattle this afternoon to summer range. He was thinking about saddling up and trying to catch up with his brothers and the cattle when he decided to give the insurance company a call on his own.

He had hoped that Halley would call him right back, but when he'd spoken with her, he could tell that she was distracted. He wondered if it had something to do with Jessica's murder. Had the school counselor's alibi checked out?

Or had Sid Granger done something more to make her suspicious?

Finally, unable to wait any longer, he put in a call to Royalty Life Insurance and got an answering machine. He glanced at his watch and realized that the main office was on the East Coast and had already closed for the day. He'd waited too long.

He was about to hang up when the automated answering machine gave him the option of listening to the company's list of agents. He waited as the voice droned on and on, finally getting to the end of the alphabet and the name Agatha Wells.

Except he didn't hear the name. He thought he must have missed it and asked to hear the list again. No Agatha Wells. No Wells at all.

He'd just hung up when his cell phone rang. He saw that it was Halley and answered quickly.

"I got some information on Agatha Wells," Halley told him without preamble. "She is no longer employed by Royalty Life Insurance Company. Based on how little information the company president was willing to give me, I'd guess she was fired."

"Fired? When?"

"Apparently some time ago. As far as I could

find out, she isn't employed by anyone right now."

Colton swore under his breath. Then what the hell was she doing investigating his father? Or was that what she'd been doing last night at dinner at the ranch?

"Want to tell me what this is about?" Halley asked.

"I will later at dinner. I need to go. See you at eight." He disconnected and swung by the ranch to talk to Emma, wondering if her inviting the woman to dinner was a case of keeping her friends close and her enemies even closer.

HALLEY PARKED IN FRONT of the Granger house, noting that Millie's car wasn't parked in the yard. The garage door was open—and empty. It appeared that Millie wasn't home.

Halley climbed out of the patrol SUV, unsure exactly what she was doing here. Since finding out that it was Millie Granger who'd discovered the allegedly "lost letter," Halley hadn't been able to get it off her mind.

The evening was cool, a skim of clouds hiding the last of the sun's rays to the west. She could smell the cottonwoods and see the cotton floating through the air like snowflakes.

Halley had hoped to find Millie at home. Sid

was still in jail. It was the perfect opportunity to talk to the woman alone—and Halley had a lot of questions, beginning with the letter Jessica had written Colton.

It seemed odd that Millie wasn't around. Maybe she was trying to get Sid out of jail. Or maybe she was taking advantage of this freedom and doing something fun. The latter seemed improbable.

As she walked toward the open garage, she tried to imagine Millie doing something just for fun, let alone kicking up her heels.

Like the house, the garage was immaculate. Everything seemed to have a place along the sides and back of the garage. Someone had actually written on the wall where each item went. Rake. Clippers. Snow shovel.

Halley made the circle, coming to a stop at the only spaces along the wall that were empty. Suitcase #1. Suitcase #2. Two empty spots, one larger than the other, were dark, the area around them faded from the sun, which had bleached the color out of the wall. Apparently, the suitcases had been stored here a very long time without being used.

That niggling feeling pulled at her again as she walked around to the front of the house, mounted the stairs and knocked, even though she wasn't expecting anyone to answer. On impulse, Halley tried the knob. Locked.

Backtracking, she entered the garage again, then tried the door leading into the house. It opened. She hesitated. Without a warrant, she was breaking the law. Anything she found couldn't be used in a court of law.

But the two missing suitcases seemed like a sure sign that Millie Granger was about to take a trip. Her husband in jail, it seemed an odd time for a woman like Millie to be packing. Unless the two of them were planning to take off together.

Halley opened the door and slipped inside. The house felt cool and dark as she quickly moved through the laundry area to the living room. Her gaze went to the rattlesnake skin on the wall. She shivered and felt a premonition so strong, she almost turned around and left.

At the top of the stairs, the landing opened onto three doors. The first one she came to was closed. She tried the door, glanced in and was startled to see a figure silhouetted against the window.

Her pulse took off, heart pounding after it, before she was able to corral herself—and make sense of what she was seeing. A faceless dress form adjusted to Millie's size stood at the window draped in a half-finished housedress. It appeared that Millie made her own clothing. Like the garage, the room was inhumanly neat, everything in its place.

Halley closed the door and stepped down the hall past a bathroom to the last doorway into the master bedroom.

Like the decor downstairs, the room had a masculine feel to it. The quilt on the bed had been made from blocks of material featuring Montana animals: elk, moose, bear, deer and antelope.

On the bed were two large suitcases that she could see at a glance matched the outlines on the wall of the garage where they had been stored. Now both suitcases were open and filled haphazardly with clothing.

Halley glanced toward the open closet. Her heart began to beat harder again. The closet looked as if someone had been tearing the clothing from the hangers. What hangers hadn't fallen to the floor hung at odd angles. Only one side of the closet was in disarray. Sid's side was in perfect order, all his clothing still hanging there.

The way the clothing had been dumped in the suitcases, it looked as if Millie was running for her life.

EMMA WAS SHOCKED to hear that Aggie Wells hadn't worked for the insurance company in years and might have been fired.

"I don't understand," she told Colton when he'd broken the news.

"Neither do I. Do you have any idea where she's staying in town?"

Emma shook her head, still in shock. She thought about the self-assured woman. "I met her for a drink out at Sleeping Buffalo, but I got the impression she was staying somewhere else. Somewhere closer to the ranch." She saw Colton's expression. "In retrospect I'll admit it might not have been a good idea to meet with her. Just like inviting her to supper might have been foolhardy under the circumstances."

"You think?"

She ignored his sarcasm. Any other time she would have made him apologize. But he was right. Sometimes she acted impetuously and it blew up in her face. This was not one of those times, she hoped.

"She told me she worked for the insurance company." Emma tried to remember the exact conversation. "Or maybe she just led me to believe that, I'm not sure. I got the name of the insurance company from Hoyt, now that I think of it."

"She's trying to prove that my father killed his other wives, isn't she?" Colton said.

Emma hedged, but saw that he already had heard—probably from one of his brothers, which meant Hoyt must have told them at some point.

"I assured her your father wasn't that kind of man."

Colton laughed. "I'm sure your assurance carried a lot of weight."

"The woman is obviously misguided."

"Did she say anything else that might give you a clue as to where I could find her?"

Emma groaned, suddenly feeling more nervous than she had when Aggie Wells had told her what she was up to. "If she no longer works for the insurance company, then why would she still be after your father?"

"It's possible she could be freelancing, taking old cases in hopes of getting a percentage of any insurance company's money she retrieved for them. Kind of like a bounty hunter or a private investigator."

"Wait a minute. I just remembered something. There was a matchbook on the table. It had a name on it. I think it said Whitehorse West. Is that a motel?"

He nodded. "It's along Highway 2 and the Hi-Line on the edge of town."

"Wait a minute," she said as he started toward the door. "What are you going to do?"

"Find out what she's up to," he said over his shoulder.

"Colton," she called after him. "Be careful."

HALLEY WAS ON HER WAY downstairs, the cold and silence inside the Granger house beginning to get to her when her cell phone rang, making her jump.

She headed out of the house the same way she'd come in as she answered it.

"I thought you'd want to know." It was the deputy who had picked up Sid the night before for driving while intoxicated. "Sid Granger just made bail."

"Who bailed him out?"

"His attorney."

Not his wife. So where was Millie? She must have had to run an errand, get some money, clean out a safe deposit box, buy gas for the car. It seemed odd that she had stopped in the middle of her packing, though. Had Sid called from the jail? Had he expected Millie to post bail? When she didn't, had she been forced to call his lawyer?

Halley didn't like that scenario. That meant Sid would be headed home, already angry with his wife. What would he do when he saw the suitcases? Or had Millie decided to just take off, forget her clothes and put some distance between her and Sid and Whitehorse?

"He still seems to be pretty worked up, but we can't hold him any longer. Just wanted to warn you to watch your back in case he comes looking for you again."

Halley snapped the phone shut, realizing that she needed to move fast. It could get ugly if Sid caught her coming out of his house. As she came out of the garage, she saw the path that led around the side of the house.

She hesitated, glancing at her patrol SUV parked in front of the house. Sid would be here soon—unless he decided to stop off at the bar for a drink or two. Millie might be back at any moment as well.

But there was something Halley wanted to check out. She took the path to the backyard, pretty sure there was another path back there that led to where Jessica Granger had died.

COLTON KNEW HE HAD just enough time to drive into town and see if Aggie Wells was still staying at the Whitehorse West Motel before he had to get ready for his date.

He feared that if he put this off, the woman would skip town. More than likely she had someone she still knew at the insurance company who would tip her off that a White-horse deputy had been asking questions about her.

Everything was already planned for his date. He'd made reservations again at Northern Lights, an upscale restaurant in downtown Whitehorse for his date with Halley. He'd asked for a private table in a corner and the best bottle of champagne they had.

"Would you also like one of our flourless chocolate cakes for dessert?" the owner, Laci Cavanaugh-Duvall, had asked him with a slight chuckle.

"Whatever you suggest."

"A special date?" she'd asked.

"I hope so."

Now as he drove toward town, he studied the horizon, glad to see nothing but blue sky. He was determined that he and Halley would have a normal date tonight.

As he reached Highway 2, he turned toward Whitehorse. He hadn't gone far when he saw the motel's neon sign ahead and shifted his thoughts to Aggie Wells.

His every instinct told him that his father had good reason to fear this woman. Even after being fired, she was still determined to prove that he'd murdered his wives? Colton couldn't wait to find out her story. The woman was either a wacko or...

He slowed and turned into the motel lot, parking in front of the building marked "Office." There was only one car and two pick-ups parked in front of the dozen rooms. Even though it was summer in Montana, this part of the state didn't get a lot of tourists. The single car didn't look like a rental, but he had no idea what Aggie Wells might be driving. For all he knew, she could own one of the pickups.

"I'm looking for Agatha Wells," he told the young female clerk behind the desk. "She is staying here in your motel, right?"

"She was. She checked out last night late."

Aggie had left after having supper at the ranch?

"Did she say if she would be back? Or possibly where she was going?"

The clerk shook her head.

"I really need to talk to her. Did she leave a phone number where she could be reached? Possibly when she registered for the room?"

"I'm sorry, I can't give out that information," the clerk said.

"Can you tell me what room she was in?"

The young woman looked surprised by the request. "Number three, but she's not there."

"Have you cleaned that room yet?" He knew

it was a long shot. But he also knew that with so few guests and little help because of it, things moved slowly in Whitehorse.

"No," she said suspiciously.

"I want to rent the room—as is."

"I don't think…"

He put cash on the counter.

She looked from it to him, then shrugged.

Colton knew it was a long shot as he took the key and walked down to number three. Opening the door, he caught the stale scent of the woman's perfume. He stood for a moment just looking at the room.

The bed hadn't been made and there were several towels on the bathroom floor. He noticed a glass on the nightstand and, using a clean washcloth, wrapped it up to take to Halley for prints.

At this point, he couldn't even be sure that the woman Emma knew as Aggie Wells was who she said she was.

He stuffed the cloth-wrapped glass into his jacket pocket and took a look around the bathroom, then the rest of the motel room.

Just when he thought there was nothing more to find, he saw what looked like a scrap of paper on the floor by the bed. Stepping over and kneeling down, he discovered it was a part of a photograph. There were other pieces in the trash can next to the bed.

Colton dumped them out and fitted the torn pieces together.

With a jolt, he saw that the photo had been taken on the Chisholm Cattle Company ranch. The picture was grainy as if it had been taken from some distance, possibly with a telephoto lens.

But it had definitely been shot at the ranch—and no doubt in secret, he thought with a curse. He recognized the corral and part of the barn—and the people in the picture. The photograph had been taken within the last two weeks.

How else could Aggie Wells have taken a clandestine snapshot of Hoyt Chisholm kissing his new wife next to the barn?

Chapter Thirteen

The cottonwoods were thicker back here by the creek. Halley worked her way through them. This time of year the grass was tall, obscuring any path that had once followed the creek to Chisholm ranch property—and a spot for lovers to meet in secret.

But she had no doubt that there'd been a trail fourteen years ago, a trail that Jessica Granger had taken the night she was murdered.

It took her a while to find her way through the tall green grass and new cottonwoods along the creek bank. The evening air had grown cool, especially along the water. Cotton from the trees floated around her, scenting the growing twilight with the smell of spring.

Halley stopped suddenly to listen. She'd thought she'd heard a rustling in the grass and brush behind her, but could now hear only the breeze stirring the leaves and the soft babble of the creek beside her.

She felt jumpy. The last of the day's sunlight flickered down through the leaves into the deep shade beneath the trees. Working her way north, she continued to push through the lush grass. She was forced to move away from the creek to circumvent a thick stand of cottonwoods, but she hadn't gone far when she found what had once been a path.

It wound through the trees in sight of the creek. Halley moved a little faster. Sid was out on bail. Millie might come back. Both would see her patrol SUV parked out front. The last thing Halley wanted to do was get Sid riled up.

The only sound was the swish of her jeaned legs pushing through the grass and an occasional cricket chirp or the cry of a hawk soaring overhead. She couldn't turn back now. She had to follow this path and prove to herself that Jessica could have come this way that night.

Where the creek turned, Halley felt confused about where she was for a moment. With the sun down, she couldn't tell if she was still going in the right direction. She found a shallow spot to wade across, soaking her boots. Is this where Jessica had crossed? What if the water had been deeper?

Halley moved faster, feeling time slipping through her fingers. It was dark in the trees now and she feared she was lost. When she came to a barbed-wire fence that marked Chisholm property, she realized that this might all have been a waste of time.

Surely Jessica didn't have to crawl through the barbed wire every time she met Colton out here. Maybe she had gotten a ride and taken the road in. Maybe Halley was dead wrong.

Now, forced to bushwhack her way through the thick grass and dense stand of small new trees growing up on this side of the creek, Halley knew that if she was right, there had to be another way in here.

She was ready to give up when she burst out of a stand of thick brush into a small opening she recognized and was grateful that at least she wasn't as lost as she'd thought.

The twilight cast an eerie, pale light over the spot where Jessica's remains had been found. Halley's heart began to pound. She'd been right. Fourteen years ago there had been a trail of sorts making this spot well within walking distance from Jessica's house.

That night Jessica had pretended to go to her room, but she must have snuck out and headed for this spot to meet, first, Hoyt Chisholm, and then wait for Colton? Or had there been someone else she'd been waiting for besides Colton? Someone she was meeting first?

COLTON DIDN'T HAVE MUCH TIME, but he had to make sure that Aggie Wells was long gone. It took another $50, but he managed to talk the motel clerk into giving him a copy of the registration form the woman had filled out.

"Do you remember what kind of car she was driving?" he asked, noting that the plates started with a three, which indicated it had come from Billings. Billings also had the closest airport to Whitehorse. He was betting the car was a rental.

"White or tan. I have no idea what kind. They all look the same to me, you know medium-sized, kind of ugly."

He did know. "Did you happen to see a rental sticker on it?"

She started to shake her head, but stopped abruptly. "I did," she said, showing the first sign of excitement. She rattled off the name on the sticker.

It took a few calls and as plausible a story as he could come up with, but he finally was told that Aggie Wells had planned to return her car today before four, but hadn't shown.

"Did she ask about a shuttle to the airport?"

"As a matter of fact, she did. I believe she said she had a six-thirty flight."

"She probably didn't mention to where."

"Actually, she did. Phoenix. I remember because I used to live there. I said, 'Bet it's changed a lot since I lived there five years ago.' And she said, 'I wouldn't know. I'm only visiting. There is no place I call home anymore.' I thought that was a little strange."

"Not if you know Aggie," Colton said and hung up.

Why Phoenix? And why didn't she make her flight? Was she still around Whitehorse?

Glancing at his watch, he headed for his house to get ready for his date. He couldn't wait to see Halley.

But as he drove down the main drag, he saw Sid Granger coming out of the liquor store and turned into an empty space next to the curb.

Sid didn't see him until Colton was almost on top of him. He looked up in surprise. Clearly, he had other things on his mind as he clutched the bottle-shaped brown paper bag in his hands and stepped to the driver's-side door of his older-model car.

The man looked awful as he squinted at Colton. "What do *you* want?" Sid snapped as he reached into his pocket for his car keys.

"I want to see you go to hell for what you did to Jessica."

"I'm already in hell." Sid fumbled with his keys, his hands visibly shaking.

"You're going to pay for what you've done—one way or the other."

The older man quit fighting to get his key into the lock and turned to look at Colton. He let out a humorless laugh. "I'm already paying in ways you can't even imagine. Everything I've ever loved has been taken away from me. *Everything*."

With that he jammed the key into the lock and opened his door, shoving Colton back as he slid behind the wheel. The engine roared and he drove off.

The last thing Colton saw was the hard lines of the man's grimacing face. He realized that Sid Granger was crying—and apparently about to get very drunk if the size of the liquor bottle was any indication.

LOSING LIGHT, HALLEY looked around for another way back to the house. She'd heard a car just moments before and feared that Sid could be home by now and had found the suitcases Millie was packing. Halley hated to think what he might do. She could only hope Millie had taken off without her clothing and hadn't come back. Either way, her patrol car was parked in front of their house. Maybe seeing the patrol car would make Sid think twice before he took his anger out on Millie.

As she looked around, she saw an opening between the trees and took it. The route turned out to be the right one. When she reached the creek, she found where someone had laid an old board across the rocks, forming a make-shift bridge.

Halley felt as if she was following in Jessica's footsteps as she crossed on the weathered gray board, then saw the remains of an old trail through the grass.

Hurrying along the trail through the tall grass, she thought she heard something coming through the grass in the distance, but when she stopped, she heard nothing. Halley hated the spooked feeling that settled inside her.

She reminded herself that the sound could have come from one of the many deer in the area. Or something even smaller. It didn't mean she wasn't alone out here. So why was her heart racing faster as she began to run, brushing at tree limbs and fighting the grass that grasped at her jean-clad legs.

At the barbed-wire fence property boundary, she stopped to catch her breath. It was getting darker here under the trees and the air had cooled considerably. Halley told herself that she was acting silly. But still she couldn't shake the bad feeling. All she wanted to do now was get back to the Granger house.

Bushes had grown up along the old rusted barbed-wire fence, but at one low spot, someone had laid a large log over the fence, forcing it down next to a boulder—and making it easy to step over.

It appeared that Jessica had used this path often. But had it been to meet Colton? Or someone else? How many others had there been? Halley felt a deep sadness at the thought—and all of it had happened not far from her own home. If Sid had caught her—

As Halley started to step over the fence, the hem of her jeans caught on a strand of barbed wire. She bent to free it and saw a small torn piece of cloth fluttering in the breeze inches away, where someone else had gotten their clothing caught in the barbs.

The cloth was faded, the pattern hardly visible anymore, but, with a jolt, Halley realized that the scrap of fabric had dark spots on it. Blood? Her pulse began to drum as she realized where she'd seen the tiny print fabric before.

With her blood pounding in her ears, she barely heard the whisper of a sound behind her. She got her hand to her weapon at her hip as she turned, but it was too late to avoid the blow. The butt of a gun caught her in the temple, dropping her to her knees. She saw the barrel pointed down at her, the metal catching the last of the light.

A fleeting thought whizzed past. She was going to be late for her date with Colton. Again. As darkness crowded her vision, she fell face-first into the tall grass at her attacker's feet.

Chapter Fourteen

Halley opened her eyes to a fierce headache and a blinding bright light. She blinked and tried to turn her head.

"Did you really think I was going to let you mess up everything?" a female voice said from the dark of the trees.

Halley lay in the grass, tree limbs forming black patterns against the twilight. She held her hand up to shield her eyes from the strong beam of light and thought she must be losing her mind. The voice had sounded like...

Millie Granger lowered the flashlight and stepped over to her. Halley would have thought the woman had come to save her except for the pistol in her right hand, the flashlight in the other. The light now made a pool next to where Halley lay on the ground.

"Millie?" She couldn't keep the surprise from her voice. As she sat up, she rubbed the bump on her head with one hand and reached for her weapon with the other. The gun was gone, her holster empty.

She looked up at Millie Granger again, everything coming back to her. The butt of a gun slamming into her skull, hearing someone behind her, finding the blood-splattered scrap of fabric caught on the barbed-wire fence near Colton and Jessica's secret spot.

She'd recognized the tiny print fabric from that first day she and Colton had stopped by the Grangers'. Millie had been wearing that old faded apron, clearly a favorite, even though it had a tear in the fabric that had left a hole. She'd been nervously toying with the hole.

"I tried to help you solve this," Millie Granger said. "I practically handed the killer over to you, but you just couldn't leave it alone, could you?"

Halley stared up at her, trying to make sense of everything. Her head ached and she felt ill. She wondered how much time she'd lost. When she glanced at her watch, she was surprised that it had only been a few minutes.

"*Sid,*" Millie said as if Halley was stupid. "He was obsessed with Jessica and determined that she wouldn't turn out like my sister. He tried to beat it out of Jessica, but when he found out she was pregnant and followed her to that awful spot where she met the men, he killed her in one of his rages. I would have come forward, but he told me he would kill me, too."

"I don't think so."

Millie laughed. "Yes, I guess it is too late to sell you on that theory, isn't it?"

Halley stared at Millie. She seemed so different, no longer pretending to be the poor, frightened, beaten-down wife who lived in terror of her husband's temper.

"So it was all a lie to make Sid look guilty," she said. "You knew I would think he'd done it. You've been leading me there all along. You purposely worked him up so he would come over to my house last night after he'd been drinking."

Her smile broadened. "Very good. I knew it the first time you came to my house. I thought to myself—that woman is too smart for her own good. Too bad, too. You could have saved yourself a lot of trouble if you'd stayed home tonight. Maybe went out with your boyfriend. But you had to come over here, didn't you? What exactly were you expecting to find?"

"Evidence that would make your husband look even more guilty. That's right. You blew it, Millie. The school counselor's alibi checked out. Sid Granger was my number one suspect."

COLTON KNEW HE WAS running a little early as he pulled down the road to Halley's farmhouse. He'd dressed in his best boots, his favorite Western shirt and his newest jeans.

When he'd stopped by the ranch to give his dad and Emma the update on Aggie Wells, they'd both raised an eyebrow.

"Another date with Halley?" Emma had asked.

He couldn't help himself—he'd grinned and changed the subject to Aggie Wells.

"She didn't turn in her rental car?" his dad asked, sounding worried.

"She must have gotten word that we were checking on her employment and just took off rather than catch her flight," Colton said. "Any idea on why she was headed for Phoenix?"

Hoyt shook his head.

"Dad, if there is anything you want to tell me…" Colton said after Emma had left the room.

Hoyt looked up at his son. His face softened. "I have tried to spare you and your brothers from all this."

"I know you had nothing to do with anyone's death or disappearance. Why, though, is Aggie Wells so convinced that you did?"

His father shook his head. "I have no idea, but I'm worried about Emma. I'm afraid something might happen to her if I don't get her away from this ranch."

Colton had wanted to question his father more, but Emma had come back into the room just then to announce that Celeste was about to serve supper. He heard his brothers coming in through the back door and, telling his father he would talk to him later, left.

Now all he wanted to do was put everything out of his mind except for Halley. But as he pulled into the yard, he realized that Halley's patrol SUV was nowhere to be seen. He glanced at his watch, surprised that she was running late again and disappointed as he cut his engine to wait.

Colton tried not to worry, yet he couldn't forget Sid Granger with a bottle of liquor and out of jail. He told himself that as long as Halley didn't cross paths with him, she would be fine.

"You really did think Sid killed her?" Millie asked.

Halley nodded. "I thought it was Sid, but then I remembered that apron you were wearing, the yellow one with the small print? I noticed that first day that it had a ragged hole in it, as if you'd caught it on something. You were kneading your fingers in and out of the hole."

Millie looked regretful. "I should have thrown the old thing away, but it was the last of my mother's and one of her favorites."

"What I don't understand is why you were wearing it that night."

"I had to leave the house quickly because Sid came home before I expected him that night. He just assumed my friend had already picked me up to take me to the Whitehorse Sewing Circle. I was forced to hide out here in the woods." She frowned. "I don't know how you came to the conclusion that I was wearing it that night, but you'll never get a DNA sample from that apron. I washed all the blood out of it years ago."

"Why did you kill her?" Halley asked, not about to tell her about the scrap of fabric caught on the barbed-wire fence. There was still the chance that this wouldn't end the way Millie was hoping it would. Even if the woman killed her, she wasn't strong enough to move her body. Maybe the crime lab would find the fabric and test the stain on it. Once they found Jessica's blood on it…

"You're wrong, and unfortunately it's going to cost you your life," Millie said and glanced at her watch in the glow of the flashlight. "Sid is out of jail. He is furious and probably already getting drunk. When he comes home, he's going to knock me around—just for effect. Then, after seeing your patrol car parked in front of our house, he's going to come looking for you. You have no idea how dangerous my husband can be when he's this upset."

"He knows the truth, doesn't he? That's why you changed your plan," Halley said, realizing it was true and she knew when it had all come together for him. "I actually witnessed the moment he figured it out. It was when I accused him of putting the rattlesnake in my bed."

Millie smiled. "I thought it was a nice touch. Sid was so proud of that horrible rattlesnake skin that he'd insisted on putting over the fireplace. He likes going out and catching them. I used his equipment and went to one of the spots he's always going on about."

Halley shook her head, even though it hurt to do so. "I don't understand why you would you try to frame your own husband."

"With him in prison for multiple murders, I can finally do whatever I want without having to see his pathetic face every day."

"You hate him that much?"

"He's weak. I could have broken that girl. I could have beaten her mother's slutty ways out of her, but Sid couldn't bear it and look how it all ended."

Halley frowned. "Jessica's mother?"

WHEN COLTON'S PHONE RANG, he thought it was Halley calling to say she was running late again.

The last person he'd expected to be calling was Sid Granger.

"Is the deputy with you?" he asked the moment Colton answered.

"What?"

"I called your house and got your cell phone number. The deputy's patrol car is in front of my house. I can't find her. Or Millie."

Colton felt his heart rate spike at Sid's words—and the fear he heard in them. "No, I'm waiting for Halley. Why are you asking me... Sid?" He realized that the man had hung up.

Snapping the phone shut, he reached for the key still in the ignition, cranked the pickup's engine to life and headed for Sid Granger's house, his fear growing with each mile.

Why would Halley's patrol car be parked in front of the Granger house? She must have gone over there to talk to Millie. Now they were both missing?

His heart pounded, fear making him break

out in a cold sweat. Jessica had been afraid in that house. For all her bravado and all her exploits, she was just a girl. A girl hell-bent on running away from that house.

Colton thought of the fear he'd heard in Sid Granger's voice and remembered the broken man he'd seen coming out of the liquor store.

What the hell *had* been going on in that house fourteen years ago? And what had happened now? His every instinct told him he had to find Halley—and fast.

"JESSICA WASN'T OURS," Millie said with disgust. "She was my sister's bastard, but rather than have the whole county talking about our family any more than they already did, I let everyone believe the baby was mine. My sister was living in Billings. It was easy enough to stay down there during the last of her pregnancy, then bring the baby back as my own."

"What happened to your sister?" Halley asked, her heart in her throat.

"She did what was best for everyone. She took her own life. An overdose, the coroner said."

Halley felt sick.

"You killed them both."

"I tried to *save* them both," Millie snapped.

"You followed Jessica that night and killed her."

"I didn't have to follow her. I knew where she was going. Just as I knew she was no good. She had my sister's blood running through her veins. I saw it when she was little, the way she always had to have Sid's attention."

Halley didn't think she could be more sickened, but she was wrong. "So it was really about competing for Sid's attention."

Millie lifted a brow, her face taking on as deadly a look as the gun in her hand. "What do you know about it? I could see the devil in her the way she sashayed around, thinking she was a lot cuter than she was."

"She was just being a little girl. Is that when you started beating her?"

"Spare the rod, spoil the child."

"That what your mother taught you?" she asked, remembering the treasured apron the woman had hung on to all these years.

Millie took a menacing step toward her. "Don't you say anything bad about my mother. She was a saint. She taught me to be a *good* girl."

Halley shuddered at the look in the woman's eyes. "You didn't have to kill Jessica. She was *running away*."

"What makes you think I wasn't glad she

was running away? I wanted to be rid of that girl. After Social Services called, I knew I couldn't use my usual methods to try to keep her in line and Jessica knew it as well. She had already brought shame on me by telling everyone she was pregnant."

"Jessica *wasn't* pregnant."

"Not this time anyway. At least the lie worked in her favor, now didn't it?"

Halley thought of the $10,000 Hoyt Chisholm had given Jessica that hadn't been found yet. "You knew about the money she was extorting."

Millie laughed. "It was my idea to hit up those men who had taken advantage of her for the money. I figured if the tramp was going to lie, why not make it worthwhile?"

Halley was at a loss for words. "If you wanted to get rid of her and she was running away that night, then why did you have to kill her?" The reason came in a flash. "The money. You wanted it for yourself so you could leave, too."

She didn't deny it.

"The letters you told your husband came from Jessica…"

"Have you ever quilted? It's a wonderful hobby. And with the internet you can talk to quilters all over the world. Isn't that amazing?

And they are such nice people. They would do anything for you."

"You had quilters mail the letters for you."

"I needed Sid to believe she was still alive until I was ready for him to find out differently."

"The lost letter," Halley said. It had started all the events in motion. "How did you get the letter?"

"Jessica confessed that in a weak moment she'd mailed the letter to Colton just in case his father didn't come up with the $10,000. It would have only complicated things. I followed the mailman the next day. The Chisholm mailbox isn't within sight of the ranch house. It was easy to get the letter back. At first I was simply going to destroy it."

"But you thought of a better way to use it by implicating Colton."

Millie smiled again. "I knew how Sid would react if he thought Colton had killed Jessica. The plan was perfect."

"You dug up Jessica's purse so he would find it."

The woman cocked her head as if listening. Halley realized that Millie hadn't been telling her all this to get it off her chest or the relieve her guilt. She'd been waiting for someone.

"You think you have it all figured out,"

Millie said distractedly. "There is just one piece of the puzzle that doesn't quite fit."

"What piece is that?" Halley asked, her heart again in her throat.

"I didn't kill Jessica. Here's your killer now."

Halley turned, sensing at the last moment that they were no longer alone.

Chapter Fifteen

Jessica's former best friend Twyla Brandon came out of the darkness, a baseball bat in her gloved hand. She stopped within swinging distance.

"I see you found Sid's bat," Millie said with a nod and smiled at the younger woman.

"Twyla?" Halley said in disbelief.

"She's the daughter I should have had," Millie said. "Jessica was a terrible friend to Twyla. She used her in the worst possible way. Fortunately, I was there for her. She'd always come to me when Jessica was bad and tell me everything. Didn't you, sweetie?"

Even with her head still aching, Halley finally saw what she'd missed before. She thought she couldn't be more horrified. "You betrayed Jessica to her mother, knowing what Millie would do to her?"

Twyla looked down at the baseball bat in her hands. "I merely told the truth." When she raised her gaze, Halley saw the hatred reflected in the light from the flashlight beam. "Jessica used me in her warped, evil game. She thought it was so funny pretending I was the one who was the tramp. Do you have any idea what her lies cost me?"

"You could have stopped her."

Twyla snorted. "No one could stop Jessica. I begged her to quit telling stories about me, but she just laughed."

"I thought you both laughed at Colton's expense," Halley said. "You could have told him the truth." But even as Halley said it, she knew Colton wouldn't have believed her. He saw what he wanted to see in Jessica—a girl in trouble he thought he could help.

"You don't know the way he always looked at me, as if I was dirt under his feet," Twyla said. "Other people heard the stories and they believed them. If it hadn't been for Millie, I don't know what I would have done."

Halley looked from Twyla to Millie and back. "She got you to kill Jessica?"

"It had to be done," Millie said. "Twyla needed to do it. I couldn't take that away from her. Jessica had to be stopped."

It turned Halley's stomach at how sick the relationship was between these two women. "Millie used you. She's still using you. You think Jessica did a number on you? Well, it was nothing compared to what this woman has done to you."

Millie laughed. "Save your breath. Twyla knows what's at stake here. She has a family and children now. She can't let you ruin her life, and you will if we let you go. No one can understand what this poor young woman has been through but me." She nodded to Twyla, who stepped closer and raised the bat.

As COLTON DROVE UP into the Grangers' yard, he caught what he realized was a flashlight beam moving through the trees along the creek. Sid was heading north along the creek through the darkness.

Colton grabbed the pistol he kept under the seat and a flashlight and leaped from his pickup. At the creek, he followed the faint light flickering through the trees from Sid's flashlight, opting not to use his own. He could hear Sid ahead of him, moving fast.

Colton didn't need to wonder where he was headed. He tucked the pistol into his jeans and followed, unnerved to realize that Sid Granger had to have known about the secret spot where his daughter used to sneak off to.

How long had he known? There was no way of knowing. Just as there was no way of knowing if Sid was leading him into a trap.

He gave little thought to that prospect. He had to find Halley. Every instinct told him she was in serious trouble, as he followed the man, moving swiftly through the tall green grass and dense cottonwoods.

Colton felt his anxiety growing. Why had Halley come to the Grangers'? Had she also found this old trail and taken it to the secret spot on the creek where Jessica had died?

He heard Sid slow ahead of him. Suddenly, the light ahead was snuffed out. He could no longer hear Sid moving through the grass and brush. He froze in midstep and listened. Darkness settled in around him along with a deathly stillness. Beyond the faint sound of the creek and the breeze in the leaves of the towering cottonwoods, he heard voices.

Then Sid was moving again, sounding as if he was running, the flashlight beam bobbing erratically, then water splashed and he heard a gunshot fill the air, then the boom of a shotgun and a cry that sent a flock of birds scattering from a treetop overhead.

Colton snapped on his flashlight and raced toward the horrible sound.

LIKE THE LAST TERRIFYING moment Halley remembered, this one happened just as fast. Twyla raised the bat and swung. Halley rolled, throwing herself toward the young woman, and only caught part of the blow on her calf. She grabbed at Twyla's legs and brought her down, scrambling to gain control of the bat, all the while knowing that Millie still held a pistol on her and that any moment she would feel the heat of lead ripping through her body.

Halley felt the cramping pain in her calf where the bat connected as she grappled with Twyla. The young woman was stronger than she looked and when Halley heard the gunshot she winced, expecting to feel the fiery pain. But instead, she saw Sid and heard his cry of pain from where Millie had shot him. He was still standing at the edge of the barbed-wire fence. He raised the shotgun in his hands, pointed it at his wife. Halley saw then that his pain had nothing to do with his gunshot wound but with what he was about to do.

He fired the shotgun and Millie let out the most eerie, horrible cry Halley had ever heard. The flashlight fell to the ground, the beam pointing at an angle that threw light on the pistol still in her one hand, the other hand cupping her stomach, which flowed dark red.

Losing her focus for just an instant, Halley

felt Twyla slip out of her grip and grab for the baseball bat lying in the deep grass. Halley tried to get to her feet, but the cramp in her calf slowed her down just long enough for Twyla to reach the bat, and she was up and swinging it.

Sid grabbed the bat, wrenching it from Twyla before she could complete her swing and throwing it into the brush out of sight. Using the shotgun like a crutch, he took a step toward Millie.

He never reached her. He collapsed to the ground just few feet shy of her, dropping the shotgun.

Halley dived for the shotgun, but Twyla got there first. In the light from Millie's fallen flashlight, Halley saw a gleam come into Twyla's eyes and realized that the woman wasn't seeing her—she was seeing Jessica, the friend who had tormented her in the most terrible way of all.

Colton came out of the darkness at a run, tackling Twyla and throwing her to the ground. Halley grabbed the shotgun and spun around.

Millie had dropped to her knees in the grass. She still had the gun in her hand, but her gaze was on the blood pouring out of her abdomen.

"Drop the gun!" Halley ordered, aiming the loaded shotgun at her.

Millie Granger slowly raised her head. She started to raise the pistol, but all the life seemed to drain out of her. She fell face forward into the grass. Behind her, Colton restrained Twyla Brandon who was crying hysterically and trying to get to Millie. Both Millie and Sid lay dead in the grass just yards from where Jessica had died.

Halley retrieved her weapon from Millie's jacket pocket, then turning to Twyla she took out her handcuffs and began to read the woman her rights.

It wasn't until later, the crime scene secured, the coroner come and gone, and Twyla safely behind bars, that Halley fell into Colton Chisholm's arms, but by then the sun was up and their second date was officially over.

Colton had sworn he was going to take it slow, but he blurted it out because he couldn't go another instant without telling her.

"I love you."

She smiled, a slow, sexy smile. "About time you realized that."

He laughed and gently touched her face as he looked into her big brown eyes. "You are so beautiful, but you know what I love about you most?"

"My sense of humor?"

He shook his head. "Your strength. You're quite the woman, Halley Robinson."

She stepped to him. "I love you, too," she whispered, and kissed him. "I always have."

Epilogue

Emma stared out the window at the wide open spaces that had filled her with such calm when she'd come to the ranch just weeks before. But she'd been a newlywed, happy and content and pinching herself at her good luck.

Now the sprawling ranch and the endless prairie seemed to echo the isolation of the Chisholm Cattle Company ranch. It hadn't helped that Hoyt had sensed her unease and hung around the house, instead of riding off with his sons.

A quiet tenseness had settled over them, as if they were both waiting for the other shoe to drop, and Emma knew it had to stop—one way or the other—as she heard her husband join her at the window.

"You need to get back to running this ranch," she said without looking at him. "I'll be fine."

"Trying to run me off, are you?" he joked,

then sobered. "Or are you afraid of being alone here with me?"

Emma turned then to look into her husband's handsome face. She touched his cheek, loving that weathered face. An honest face, her mother would have called it.

"I could never be afraid of you," she said softly. She would never believe he had anything to do with the death of two of his wives or the disappearance of the third, no matter what anyone said or thought.

Hoyt didn't look convinced, as he took her hand and brought it to his lips. "Maybe I'm afraid for you."

Emma shook her head, smiling up at him. "There is nothing to fear as long as we're together."

They hadn't heard anymore from Aggie Wells since they'd discovered she had been fired from the insurance company she worked for. Hoyt had talked to her boss. He'd apologized and suggested that Hoyt get a restraining order if Aggie contacted him again.

But Emma knew Hoyt wasn't going to do that. Like her, he was just hoping the woman was gone from their lives.

"Now get out of here," Emma said. "I need to plan a special supper for tonight. Colton is bringing Halley."

Hoyt shook his head in mild amusement. "You think it's serious?"

Emma nodded, unable to hide her pleasure. "Halley is perfect for him."

"So you say." He glanced over at her and she saw the suspicion in his gaze. "You didn't have anything to do with that, did you?"

"Me?" she asked innocently. "Oh, did I mention that I also invited that nice young woman who just returned from college at Montana State University. Graduated in animal husbandry. I think she went to school with Dawson. She'd come home to help her father run their ranch."

"Emma..."

HALLEY SAT ON HER HORSE, looking out over the prairie. "You're right, this view is amazing," she said. The breeze stirred her hair, which hung loose over her shoulders. She turned her face up to the warm sunlight and breathed in the fresh scent of pine and summer.

On the horse beside her, Colton was looking at her, rather than the view. She could feel the warmth of his gaze, hotter than the sun overhead. Halley smiled to herself, remembering their third date. It had seemed as if it was never going to happen, given the way their other dates had gone.

It had been so clear that Colton wanted to do this right with her. She loved that about him. No more frogs down the neck, but she definitely had his attention.

They'd gone to dinner at Northern Lights, the nicest restaurant in Whitehorse, had champagne and candlelight. It wasn't until they were on the way home that they both had started laughing at the same time.

"That was so not us," Halley got out between laughs.

"Could it have been more awkward?" Colton agreed. He'd stopped laughing and had slowed the pickup. "You and I—"

"We don't fit the mold. Pull over."

He shot her an amused look, then pulled over onto a dirt road, coming to stop on a small rise out of sight of the highway. He put down his window and shut off the engine. No full moon, only a sliver on the horizon and a few scattered stars glittering above them.

"I wanted everything to be perfect our first time," he said, putting his arm around her.

"It *is* perfect," she whispered and he kissed her.

It *had* been perfect. They'd made love in the cab of his pickup—just like high school kids—and when they came up for air, the sky was ablaze with the real Northern Lights.

They'd talked and laughed, lying in each other's arms, their feet sticking out the open window of the pickup. That's when Halley knew with certainty that this was the man for her.

"Colton?" She blinked and saw that Colten had gotten off his horse. He was standing next to hers, holding her reins and looking up at her with such love in his eyes that her heart took off at a gallop.

"Do you know why I brought you up here?"

Her heart raced a little faster. "You said it was to have the lunch that Emma packed. I love Emma's food, so you'd better not be fooling with me."

He grinned, his brown eyes golden in the sunlight. He had his Stetson pushed back. The man couldn't have been more handsome, nor could she have loved him more than she did at that moment.

COLTON HAD PROMISED HIMSELF he was going to take it slow, but there was nothing slow about the beat of his heart when he was around this woman. He'd been drawn to her ever since they were kids. Now they'd been brought back together and he wasn't going to let anything keep them apart, if he could help it.

"Halley?"

"Yes, Colton?"

He looked into her big brown eyes. His heart pounded like a war drum. "Marry me?"

Tears filled her eyes and for one heart-stopping moment, he thought she was going to say no. He watched her bite her lower lip as she fought to hold back the tears. "Oh, yes!"

He lifted her out of the saddle and into his arms. "I love you, Halley Robinson."

She brushed at her tears. "I love you, too," she said on a ragged breath, then looked down at what he held out to her.

It was corny and clichéd, right down to the small velvet box, but some traditions felt right.

Halley's fingers trembled as she opened the box. She let out a pleased sound, her face lighting up at the beautiful Montana agate engagement ring.

"Oh, Colton," was all she said as he slipped it on her finger. She threw herself into his arms. Emma's wonderful lunch forgotten until later that afternoon when they sat on the edge of the ridge watching the afternoon sun dip behind the Little Rockies.

Colton could imagine the excitement back at the house when he and Halley told his father and Emma the news tonight at supper. Hoyt had always said this was where Colton belonged, but he'd never felt it until this moment.

His future lay in this wild, expansive land and this woman. They would make a home here, their children would grow up on this ranch. He could see it all now. As he looked over at his beautiful bride-to-be, he knew this is the way it was always meant to be.

* * * * *